AMREVET DAYS ONE

VERA NAZARIAN

COPYRIGHT PAGE

AMREVET DAYS ONE
Vera Nazarian

Cover Art Designed by Vera Nazarian
Includes imagery provided by: Deposit Photos and MyFonts
No AI software was used in the creation of this cover or book

February 14, 2025

FIRST EDITION

Trade Hardcover - ISBN: 978-1-60762-193-5
Trade Paperback - ISBN: 978-1-60762-194-2

Published by Norilana Books
P. O. Box 209, Highgate Center, VT 05459-0209, USA
https://www.norilana.com/

Printed and bound by Ingram Lightning Source LLC.

Australia: Ingram Content Group AU Pty Ltd, Melbourne, Victoria. US: Lightning Source LLC, La Vergne, Tennessee / Allentown, Pennsylvania / Jackson, Tennessee, United States. UK: Lightning Source UK Ltd, Milton Keynes, United Kingdom. Europe: Lightning Source UK Ltd, with facilities in Germany, France, and Spain.

The authorized representative in the European Economic Area is Lightning Source France, 1 Av. Johannes Gutenberg, 78310 Maurepas, France. compliance@lightningsource.fr

AN ALIEN HONEYMOON TRAVELOGUE OF ATLANTIS!

Fans of **The Atlantis Grail** have asked for a spicy story of **Gwen** and **Aeson's** honeymoon in all its glorious detail, and here it is…

Amrevet Days is the Atlantean equivalent of a honeymoon, but taken approximately eight months after the wedding. By custom, the newlyweds must escape to a secret location to enjoy each other.

Now that Gwen is the Imperatris, married to the stunningly handsome Imperator of the most powerful nation on Atlantis, they have the entire planet at their disposal.

Come along with the happy couple and experience the joys of physical love on board a luxury flying ship, as they visit the remarkable sites of the planet, explore mysterious ancient landmarks, and learn more about one another. In addition, discover fun revelations and secrets about other favorite characters in **The Atlantis Grail** universe and what is yet to come.

The Atlantis Grail is a YA series, but this novel stands outside the sequence, due to its 18+ subject matter, and is only suitable for older audiences.

NOTE: it is strongly recommended that you read **Amrevet Days One** only *after* you've read the four books in the original series (**Qualify, Compete, Win, Survive**), or you'll miss out on all the delicious slow-burn buildup of their relationship!

AMREVET DAYS ONE is the first volume of a spicy alien honeymoon travelogue of Atlantis.

VERA NAZARIAN

An Alien Honeymoon
Travelogue of Atlantis

AMREVET
DAYS
ONE

For Teri N. Sears,
with love and endless gratitude for your friendship and
*incredible, **astra daimon** caliber technical support.*

AUTHOR'S NOTE

To All My Wonderful Readers,

You asked for a spicy and intimate look at Gwen and Aeson's relationship, and I am happy to oblige! Enjoy the Atlantean equivalent of their honeymoon, called **Amrevet Days**, in all its romantic glory.

This story is quite different from my usual intense, plot-driven action adventures with intricate, epic-scale story arcs that require very long books to properly develop.

Amrevet Days is a cozy, sensual travelogue of an alien planet, with low stakes and high spice. It is currently being serialized, a chapter at a time, on my subscription platforms (Patreon and Ream). And this naturally lends itself to easy break-off points in the plot, and blessedly shorter books.

I decided to break it up into several smaller volumes and publish them individually. This way you get the story much sooner, and in nice, digestible chunks, even if you are not one of my serial subscribers.

This first volume is called **Amrevet Days One**. Because there's going to be a **Two** and a **Three**, and so on (which you can continue to read in serialized format on my subscription platforms).

I expect there will be about 4 or 5 volumes altogether, and I will publish them all in one big omnibus book—eventually, several years down the road. When completed, the entire novel is going to be one of my typical, long and hefty books.

You might also wonder, where does this story fall in the general timeline? Technically, it is book 4.5 of **The Atlantis Grail** series. But really, it falls *after* the last chapter of **Survive** but *before* the epilogue of **Survive** (which, in turn, is followed by **The Book of Everything**).

However, because of its 18+ spice levels, I am not listing **Amrevet Days** as an official part of **The Atlantis Grail** series, which is intended for teens and young adults. **Amrevet Days** is definitely not YA, and is intended for mature audiences, hence it is "TAG-adjacent."

When should you read this book in the greater scheme of things? First, you must be an 18+ grownup. Second, please read at least the original core series (**Qualify, Compete, Win, Survive**) before you attempt to read this book.

And now, enjoy the leisurely delights!

Vera Nazarian
January 23, 2025
Vermont, USA

INTRODUCTION

Did I mention that Aeson Kassiopei, my Imperial Husband, has a big, juicy dick?

Yes, Aeson, my Aeson. Mr. Kassiopei, Archaeon Imperator of *Atlantida*, that one. And yes, I realize, none of this is suitable to go anywhere near my Book of Everything.

But I love every delicious moment of what's happening between us and so, I kind of need to write this down *somewhere*, short of screaming it into my pillow (which I kind of already do, when he takes me from behind . . . my face gets smushed into cushiony bedding with every plunge of that you-know-what, and let me tell you, he is not holding back).

Okay, I'm still blushing even to say that word, but I need to get over it.

It's not a you-know-what, it's a cock.

His *penis*. Hard and warm and so wonderfully expansive inside me. My sweet Aeson's dick, cock, penis. . . . There, I'm an adult, a married woman, I can say it.

But I'm getting ahead of myself. So let me explain: this is my private diary. I'm hoping no one gets to read this, especially not our child—not for a good, long time, at least not while I can know about it. Seriously, this is as intimate as it can get.

Incidentally, we're on our Atlantean honeymoon—our Amrevet Days. And yes, it's been months since the insanity of the alien war and the apocalyptic events.

I'm about five months pregnant, and there's already a sizeable baby belly. We actually decided to take our Amrevet Days trip *now*, precisely because of the belly. If it gets any larger, it will make it a little more awkward for all the things we are doing to each other's bodies.

All the things I'm going to describe.

But first, I need to stop blushing. It's *not* embarrassing, Gwen, you silly numbskull. It is glorious and natural and very, very *messy*. Okay, yes, that part is a little embarrassing. It's gotten so that I can't face the Imperial Palace servants who must change the Imperator's bedsheets every dratted morning. Because we make such a sticky mess.

Hence, the long anticipated Amrevet Days, where no one will care that we're having all that sex because it's what we're supposed to be doing.

And it'll give us extra time to indulge in each other, utterly and completely, before the baby comes.

So now I've started this diary, and will be scribbling in it, in between the good stuff, the sweet and erotic stuff.

Strap in for the ride, diary.

My ride and *his* ride.

Our ride.

Im amrevu.

CHAPTER 1

S o where do we end up going for our Amrevet Days? Whatever secret plans Aeson may have had earlier, to show me cosmic wonders, were ruined by the fact that so many Hel system space stations were destroyed in the alien war. Indeed, the Atlanteans have just barely started the international rebuilding process around Rah, Septu, Tammuz, and the grand restoration of Ishtar Station (which was not completely destroyed but suffered major damage).

Our visit to those outposts will just have to wait. And besides, as I tell Aeson, I've had just about enough "space exploration" to last me a few years (and if I'm honest, a lifetime —but I don't admit that out loud, in case I feel differently months or years down the road).

"In that case, *im amrevu*, we're going to stay closer to the ground," he tells me with a mischievous look. And then he presents me with this much better alternative, to which I immediately respond with a huge, excited "yes!"

We're taking a private *nubu depet*—which translates as "gold boat," a kind of hovering luxury yacht, the size of a multi-story estate—to fly around the globe and secretly visit multiple picturesque locales. For the next few months, we're going to be everywhere—not only in Imperial *Atlantida* but all around the surface of the planet Atlantis. We're going to see stunning scenery, waterfalls, gorgeous beaches, mountains, forests, even exciting urban centers in different countries. We'll visit the native sites and attractions, sample the local delicacies, and spend a lot of even more luscious carnal time with one another.

As tradition goes, we're not announcing our itinerary to anyone. But because we're Imperial Kassiopei, and we don't want to start an international incident, certain nations and heads of state will be informed in advance, so that proper diplomatic permissions and security precautions can be set in place.

It is also unavoidable that our *nubu depet* will have Imperial guards, plus a staff of servants, and even a medical team, just in case (with me being pregnant, Aeson insists). But Aeson tells me they will all keep out of our way, and our surroundings will be tasteful and discreet, with guaranteed privacy intended for *our pleasure*.

Someone will have to change those sheets, I think again, with a rush of heat in my head. *Someone will hear the sounds we make . . . the rhythmic thudding of furniture . . . his deep groans just before orgasm, my own high-pitched cries as I come . . . over and over.*

"Don't worry about anything," he tells me on Yellow Ghost Moon 21, 9771, the night before we begin our romantic journey, while we're still at our Imperial Palace Quarters. It's long past eleventh hour of Khe, it's been a long day, and we're finally alone in the Imperator's master bedroom.

I pause contemplatively and glance at the star-filled night outside the great arched windows. I observe the tiny silver disk that is Pegasus near zenith, and great violet Amrevet just rising over the horizon, visible like a lantern through the shade of inky lacework that is the park greenery far below. With an intimate look, Aeson steps close to me and captures one of my hands with his own. Almost unconsciously he rubs the inside of my wrist, then brings it up for a lingering pulse kiss. . . .

So warm and strong. . . . At his touch, a tingling sensation of electricity floods me, and I shudder with immediate arousal. The pressure of his mouth over my pulse points never fails to send an almost painful stab of desire through me. Indeed, at this point in my pregnancy—now that the morning sickness, bloating, and nausea have abated—I've discovered a heightened craving for physical intimacy with him.

"You realize," he says with an amused expression, probably noticing my widened, receptive eyes, "the *nubu depet* staff are impeccably trained. They know they must be invisible. And the walls are quite good at—masking noise."

I shake my head with a weak laugh, then place my other arm around his neck and stroke the back of his head, the silken gold of his Kassiopei hair, with my fingertips. "You know, I never thought I'd be a screamer," I whisper awkwardly, leaning close to his face, with a new surge of heat. "Why am I such a screamer, Aeson?"

He chuckles, still holding my wrist. "Is that a rhetorical question?"

"Jerk! You're laughing at me."

"Never." But his lips are quivering in that same way when, out of habit, he begins to repress a reaction, to exert control over his countenance, and then recalls himself and just doesn't bother. Because—why should he now? He's the Imperator, lord of all things, and the ultimate authority, with no one in this nation to stifle his spirit. He can permit himself to *feel*, to reveal whatever hidden part of himself he wants. . . . Especially with his *amrevu* Imperial Wife.

Hence, the relaxed, quivering lips, the blooming sweet smile.

Ah, his lips, so chiseled, so. . . .

I pull my wrist out of his clutches and then use both hands to pull him in for a fierce kiss. After only a few heartbeats, his mouth takes over, covering mine. He then lifts me effortlessly (as though I'm light as a feather and not turning more and more each day into a beached whale) and in seconds we end up on the huge bed—the Imperator's bed—on top of the royal blue covers.

Blue. . . .

It's all his—*his* Imperial Blue Court, I'm reminded once again, with a kind of visceral relief. And therefore, it is mine, ours.

This bed we now occupy, it's the exact same size as the Imperial Crown Prince's bed in those *other* Quarters, a floor below—a luxury sleeping platform immense enough to fit an entire family. Or to host an ancient orgy.

A different fleeting thought comes to me. So many generations of Kassiopei were conceived in *this* bed, slept here as little children, along with their Imperial parents.

And now . . . here we are. The baby inside my belly was made downstairs, in a different bed—the same one where Aeson was probably conceived, since his grandfather was still the Imperator at that point. . . .

As usual these past few weeks, Aeson makes sure to fall on the bed first, then lies back against the pile of cushions, pulling me on top of him, so as not to put too much pressure on my abdomen. I keep telling him it's okay, but he insists that he is too heavy, and his grown man's weight might be too much for the baby. Admittedly, I miss the sensual weight of him covering me during sex, but I've stopped arguing days ago, and just allow him to pull me up.

I end up straddling him. We've kicked off our shoes, but otherwise we're still fully dressed, having come back from an intimate family *niktos* meal with Dad, Gracie, George, Devora, and Manala (Gordie couldn't make it, being stuck on a work project). It was just a few corridors down, in our favorite large living room, and completely casual, so no formal dress-up was required. A fun evening, during which we chatted about our upcoming trip and played coy with our curious family members as to where we will be. Despite being plied with probing and sneaky questions, we held our ground, laughed, and revealed nothing.

Aeson is wearing a light shirt and pants, and I have on a simple, loose, pregnancy dress. It's just a single layer of pretty lavender fabric I can pull up and over my head. Underneath, I've got a bra and sensible panties—none of that itchy lacy stuff. Good thing Aeson doesn't care about lace, only my current comfort.

He also enjoys divesting me of my underwear . . . slowly.

"How do you feel?" he asks, lifting up my dress over my head and casting it off nearby on the bed.

"Very well, especially after that nice meal," I reply, tugging gently at his silky cream shirt as I begin unbuttoning it to reveal his bronzed throat and chiseled chest.

"Not too full?" He places one palm over my slightly bulging tummy and simply rests it there lovingly, against *our baby*.

"Nope, just right," I say. "Though, knowing me, I might be really hungry again in time for Ghost meal."

He chuckles, casting a glance at the back of the room. "Not a problem. The food cabinet is well-stocked."

"Good, because I will wake up and eat half of whatever's there again." I smile and chuckle also, then pull the unbuttoned shirt all the way off him and cast it aside.

Holy crap, but my husband is gorgeously shaped. His lean abdomen, so perfectly toned, his narrow, tapering waist contrasting with the wide shoulders and span of chest, those muscular arms. . . .

I rub my hands along his skin, starting at his shoulders and moving down past his belly button to his lower abdomen. I feel every hard plane of his muscles underneath. And his male scent —he smells like complex musk.

Already, there's a prominent bulge at his crotch. The outline of his penis grows before my eyes, pushing up the fabric of his pants. But he lies back watching me with a relaxed expression, his steady gaze sliding relentlessly over parts of me. Only his breathing has deepened. And his hand, still on my belly, is starting to stroke in gentle, slow circles.

"Mmm . . ." I make a sound of pleasure at the warm feel of his large hand, which now abandons my belly and wanders higher, up and down the side of my waist, while he reaches out his other hand to fumble at the front clasp of my bra.

As he does so, I work to unfasten his pants and set *him* free.

My bra clasp is simple, like the push of a button, and it pops open, releasing my very big pregnancy breasts. I'm already pretty large in the chest as it is, and they've never been particularly perky. . . . But now, because of the baby, they seem enormous as they fall out and *down*, dangling lower than ever. Without the bra to hold them up, I feel their sudden pendulous weight. But at the same time, that sensation of loss of constraint is very sensual, especially considering what's about to happen between us.

"Oh, jeez, I've gotten so huge . . ." I mutter, momentarily looking down at myself with reproach, even as I lean over him, continuing to undo the front of his pants. My ridiculously enormous boobs swing forward, brushing at his lower abdomen, as I tug at the waistline of his pants, and then let my fingers quickly fumble at his weird Atlantean masculine underwear that opens in the front with a weird little loop-clasp. . . . I still haven't quite gotten the hang of it.

I happen to glance up into his eyes and see him ogling me, practically drooling. Ah, my husband and his love of my tits.

"No, you're perfect," he whispers, and his voice has gone deep. "But you should hurry up and let my *varqooi* out before I explode."

"Sorry, yes . . ." I mutter, and I smile, and bite my lower lip . . . even as my own breath and pulse starts to quicken with anticipation, while I feel the wetness down *there*, between my legs.

At last, his underwear yields to me and I let his big boy out.

Aeson exhales loudly as the shaft of his cock twitches and stands up immediately, long and thick, over his engorged scrotum. He is uncut, as with most Atlantean males, and the foreskin has naturally retracted over the flushed head, exposing the scalding-hot, sensitive tip.

The head of the serpent. . . .

At once I take him with both hands, gently squeezing then stroking the precious length of him, feeling his *pulse* and heat and thickness—at which point he makes another harsh sound of breath escaping—and then I sidle forward on the bed, still straddling him, to position myself just directly above.

My panties are still on me, but I simply push aside the crotch, feeling the soaking wet spot in the fabric where I've leaked my female juices. And then I rise up on my knees and come down, impaling myself on him.

As his penis slides inside me, I moan at the intense stab of pleasure that enters my core.

"My sweet Gwen," he says, taking both of my tits, one in each hand. At once I feel my nipples hardening, poking like buttons against his warm fingers.

"Are you ready?" he asks, as he caresses my nipples with his thumbs, sending pangs of electricity coursing through me. He then uses his palms to grasp and knead the rest of my plump breast flesh. Even so, he is unable to cup an entire boob completely with his large hand—yes, that's how big I've gotten.

"Yes, please," I moan, hot and swollen on the inside, *full of him*, but still not moving, keeping my back straight and only leaning in to flatten my tits against his hands. "Okay, I think I'm perfectly upright, so that my belly will not get squished once I start to bounce."

He chuckles. "Don't worry, I'm holding you. . . . I have you."

He releases my tits and this time grasps both of my hips, supporting me from underneath. I feel the steady pulse of his penis, like a stallion poised to run, and the burning warmth of arousal spreads all through the depth of my vaginal canal.

"Let's go," he says roughly. "Ride me, *im amreve*."

I place my hands on his hard, muscular torso to steady myself, and then start to rise up slowly. The initial sucking sensation as I lift upward for the first time is such exquisite pleasure that I moan at once. And then I begin the rhythmic movement, a combination of lift and circular motion, and my hips naturally fall into the grind. . . .

He starts to breathe harshly, and his strong fingers tighten over my rear, squeezing the globes of my hips as we ride together. Our delicious rhythm has been established. In it, I'm moaning loudly as I glide up and down on him, while he remains controlled and silent except for his elevated breath through clenched lips.

The world narrows. There is nothing but the hot, hard planes of his muscles beneath me—his firmament supporting my weight—and the thick heft of his shaft, slick from my natural lubrication, continuing to impale my burning core. . . .

And oh, the dark intensity of his lapis lazuli blue eyes. . . .

Whenever I'm able to look, to barely focus enough to meet his eyes, I see his pupils are dilated with arousal. He stares up at me, his gaze boring into me as much as his physical body labors inside mine.

Faster and faster I bounce, and he thrusts up slightly to meet my every movement. Even now he's careful not to go too deep, because of the baby—even though we've been told by medics it's perfectly safe.

I'm also aware he's holding back, in order to prolong the moments before he explodes inside me. Kassiopei males tend to ejaculate too quickly, and recover just as quickly, but with enough practice, my husband has achieved a remarkable stamina for the duration of a single act.

And now, he strains to hold on, giving me time to achieve my own release instead of interrupting us multiple times in the middle of an act as he comes and recovers, then comes again, over and over. . . .

I find it highly endearing.

But right now, my mind is not quite my own, as I ride him with abandon, even as the familiar pressure builds inside me. Then at last my moans become even more high-pitched, my grinding hips go into exaggerated motion of their own accord, and I am tossed by a wave. . . . He knows I'm orgasming because my vaginal walls spasm around him, and so he allows himself to come also.

I love the deep sound of his voice when he is out of control in those seconds. . . . It bottoms out, and his hard baritone groan scrapes the floor, just before he catches his breath and stiffens into silence. . . .

Then, his cock starts to pump the hot seed inside me.

When that happens, I come again, spasming around him, reveling in the sticky scalding abundance of his ejaculate which blends with my inner lube, and the excess spills out in a gooey sticky mess around our genitals and beyond.

Someone will have to clean up all of that wet bedding tomorrow.

But we'll be long gone, floating on board the luxury *nubu depet*, on our way to our first destination, on the opposite side of the world.

The hauntingly beautiful, ancient ruins just outside the city of Heruvar.

CHAPTER 2

They like to say in New Deshret that Heruvar is located in the center of the world. It definitely falls along the planet's equatorial line, similar to Poseidon's location on the opposite hemisphere. However, unlike Poseidon's surrounding fertile grasslands and forests, and the Djetatlan Ocean to the south, Heruvar is landlocked and enclosed by a harsh desert on all sides.

I've been told the climate of the surrounding area is hot, dry, and lifeless like the Sahara on Earth. But the city itself—the second largest in New Deshret after Xois, the capital—is a remarkable oasis.

All I know about it is that the Great Pyramid of Giza has been relocated there after the Games of the Atlantis Grail and permanently reassembled just outside the city in a pristine desert location, surrounded by sands.

On Earth, you could see the Giza Plateau pyramids from Cairo. And now, on Atlantis, you can see the solitary Ex-Giza Great Pyramid from Heruvar.

But we're not going there.

Indeed, after my ordeal in Stage Two of the Games, during

which I'd become intimately acquainted with far too many pyramid stones (crawling and hanging on to them for dear life, getting my hands and knuckles and other body parts scratched raw, having to embrace them and pee on them, ugh . . .) I'd like to avoid the ancient Wonder altogether.

We're going to Heruvar's opposite side. The place where this ancient city originated and grew from a single fertile spot in the vast desert until it became the sprawling urban center that it is today.

That oldest spot, currently found just beyond the outer edge of the grand metropolis, is the ruined Old City of Anun-Xaat.

It is mostly an abandoned, haunting (and supposedly haunted) place, inhabited only by city vermin and wildlife, archaeologists, and occasional curious tourists. Beautiful manmade structures rise from among overgrown hillsides. They form obelisks, shrines, tombs, and underground caverns hewn of the local *djigeet* stone.

And at the heart of it lies the Anun oasis spring, the one that gave life to this city. Its cool waters pool in a deep pond that has been ornamentally paved by human hand, and the mosaic inlay is a work of ancient art. Aqueducts run off in all directions, and more mosaic-paved channels lead the waters in an intricate maze of pools and waterfalls—hundreds of them scattered throughout the Old City.

Some of the ponds are shallow, and the waters that emerge cool from the ground are heated during the day by the scorching glare of Helios, so that they turn into warm baths by nightfall, acting like natural hot springs—except that it is not Atlantis's inner heat but the burning Helios from above that makes them so.

By morning the waters cool down, and the cycle starts again.

It is here that our *nubu depet* makes its way. Aeson and I are going to visit the waters of Anun-Xaat, and discover the picturesque desert oasis wonder.

. . .

THE DESERT of Heruvar is an endless expanse of dunes formed by striated sands of mauve, turquoise, and gold. By day they glitter and sparkle in the sun, by night they glow with phosphorus radiance, lending a voluptuous shape to the desert.

As our luxury cruise ship descends over Heruvar, I stare in amazement at the sparkling ocean of multicolored sand underneath a blazing white morning sky that fills the view port windows to the distant horizon in all directions. I turn to glance at Aeson and see him watching me in my childlike wonder.

"Do you like it, *im amrevu?*" he asks with an intimate smile.

"It's incredible!" Unconsciously, I squeeze my Imperial Husband's hand.

"Wait till we get closer," he says, his strong fingers sliding to cover mine, even as our *depet* continues falling from the sky, and the desert rushes up to meet us in a dizzying optical illusion.

We briefly see the sprawl that is the modern city, with its high-rise skyline, roofs and cupolas glittering with gold trim. Off to one side I notice the triangular shape of the Great Pyramid looming to the North. And then, in an instant, it's gone, as the cityscape view overtakes the horizon.

But our *depet* slows down only when we reach the Southern edge, and the residential districts give way to overgrown ruins. It comes to a smooth hover stop a few feet above ancient street level in the middle of nowhere.

"Ready to go?" Aeson says, after informing our discreet staff via his wrist unit. And we emerge from our luxury bedroom into empty corridors (the staff has dispersed politely to give us our privacy), make our way down two deck levels to the boarding airlock, and then take the comfortable exit ramp to step into the hot air outside.

The heat strikes us like an oven. And the sky is brilliant and blinding. I'm wearing shaded contact lenses, super sunscreen, and even Aeson has put on sunglasses in this deadly radiance.

We're both clad in sandals and long and loose white clothing reminiscent of the desert nomad tribes of Earth. The fabric breathes and drapes us lightly, and we're wearing little else underneath. I've a scarf wrapped around my head, and Aeson wears a head covering similar to the traditional Khepresh, except it is unadorned white. He also carries a sizable backpack with food and drink and other supplies for us to have a picnic at some point.

We begin walking slowly, marveling at the surroundings. There is silence, greenery of climbing vines, bright sudden flowers emerging from the rocks and sandy soil, elegant remains of ancient structures, and the desert wind making strange music around us.

"Look!" Aeson points to a glittering pond of water in a small rounded basin, only a few steps before us. "The aqueduct network begins here."

Oh, wow. . . .

Sure enough, I notice that the basin connects to a long and narrow stone-lined channel that runs off and continues indefinitely, branching off into more waterways and reservoirs. And as I look beyond it, there is no end to the maze of water, all of it glittering in random surprising spots between the ruins.

"Oh, this is incredible," I repeat, rising a palm to shield my eyes from the glare. "How far does it go?"

"For a *mag-heitar*, or so."

A *mag-heitar* is ten kilometers. My mouth falls open stupidly. "My Dad must see this!"

"He's likely seen it already," Aeson replies with amusement.

Charles Lark, my father, was a professor of classics and antiquity back on Earth. Here on Atlantis, he currently works at the Imperial Poseidon Museum as a researcher and lecturer. And it's indeed possible that he's at least been made aware of this archeological site, even if he hasn't yet visited it.

"Come," Aeson tells me, taking my hand. "I want to show you something in particular. It's not too far from here, and an excellent place to rest."

"But I'm not tired," I retort.

"You will be." He glances at me and raises one brow.

"What's that supposed to mean?" I tap his arm, starting to laugh.

"You'll see."

"Ooh! Okay. Then lead on, my Imperial Sovereign." I giggle and mock this man who is the Imperator of Imperial *Atlantida*. Yes, I have no shame.

But Aeson wraps one arm around me from the back of my waist, and pulls me in close to him. His roving hand continues downward and he squeezes my rump, lingering there sensually, while he leans down to kiss me warmly on the lips.

At once, I feel breathless. An unexpected stab of arousal passes through me at the feel of his mouth hard against mine, not to mention his aggressive hold on my behind. He then captures my hand again, and off we go.

WE FOLLOW the endless water channels, ponds, and basins for at least a quarter of an hour, moving toward a growing source of noise up ahead, and arrive at last at what looks to be an unusual, tiny island situated in the center of a small but strongly churning lake. But when we approach, I realize the lake is actually a horseshoe shape, a kind of large, semi-circle pond, paved in the same glorious mosaic, and it hugs a rocky formation with a raging waterfall.

Crystal-clear water cascades with loud violence, emerging directly from the top of the rocks, hitting three outcrop tiers, and it churns into foam at the bottom, creating the lake.

"Aeson, it's so powerful! And beautiful!" I say, breathing in wonder, as we stand before the rim of the frothing pond, feeling the foam spray cool us even here.

"This is the ancient freshwater Anun Spring," he says, taking his sunglasses off and leaning into the cool spray. "It's the source of all life in Heruvar. It was here at the time of Landing, and who knows how much longer before that."

"Are you saying this spring is over nine thousand Atlantean years old?" I put one hand to my mouth. "How is that even possible? A single little spring? Wouldn't it have dried out ages ago?"

Aeson chuckles. "A normal spring or a well would. But this spring hits deep. It goes incredibly far down, directly into a great water table underneath the planetary crust—a freshwater ocean in the mantle. The measured water pressure is very powerful, and it's part of the reason the ancients built this fascinating network of paved water aqueducts—all of it to keep the water from forming a lake or even a sea which would be wasteful and evaporate a great deal—and instead controlling its flow above ground."

He takes another step forward, closing his eyes, and the spray dances on his bronzed skin, forming tiny beads on his long dark lashes. I step closer also, then bend down and put my hand into the water.

The pressure of the ice-cold water hits my fingers with unexpected strength, stinging my skin like needles.

Momentarily, it feels like my hand is being ripped away.

"Oww!" I exclaim and pull back, feeling my hand still stinging.

"Careful!" Aeson says. "Very powerful flow here, near the source."

"Good thing I didn't step into it," I say.

"No, that wouldn't be a good idea." He gives me an amused glance and then turns to look around us, as if searching for something. "There. . . ." He points to an area beyond the lake where several narrow channels run off to form an endless series of round pools, receding into the distance like beads on a string —where each bead is a pool, and the string between them is a waterway channel.

"If you want to soak your feet or even take a dip, those are perfect. In fact—" He smiles at me meaningfully.

"What?" I look back at him coyly.

"I think you and I are going to take a dip," he says. "I admit, it's why I brought you here."

"Not to show me the amazing Anun Spring?"

"That was just an excuse." His smile, his whole expression turns deliciously wicked. "I had ulterior motives."

I feel my mouth curve into an involuntary smile. Ahhh . . . my sneaky Husband knows just the best things to say. "All right," I whisper mockingly. "Show me your ulterior motive."

Aeson and I walk away from the waterfall and lake, following its aqueducts toward the bead necklace of pools. As we approach, I see their considerable size and that each one is a shallow pond of about a hundred feet in diameter with a stone floor of gorgeous mosaic artwork. The water is barely moving, lapping against the basin edges, as the hot wind creates occasional tiny ripples on its mirror-smooth surface.

Aeson leans before the rim of one and puts his tanned hand into the gentle water. "This one is good," he says. "Go on, try it."

I dip my hand into the water, and oh! The liquid is smooth, almost calm, with only a mild current underneath the surface. Instead of freezing, it is barely lukewarm. "Oh! Yes, this is very nice," I say.

In reply, Aeson sets the pack down on the ground and then begins removing his light robe.

"What are you doing?" I laugh.

"Take your clothes off, *im amrevu*," he says, stopping momentarily, and the look in his darkened eyes is unmistakable.

"What if someone sees us?" I ask bashfully, looking around at our silent surroundings and the distant sound of the waterfall.

He laughs, his deep voice in its wickedness turning me to melted jelly. "Do you see anyone?"

"Um, no. Ancient ghosts? Okay. . . ." I giggle. And then I start removing my own robe.

In an instant, we divest ourselves of our outer clothing and head gear, laying them on the rim of the pool. I am once again in a bra and panties, with my prominent tummy showing. My hair was pinned up in a careless messy bun underneath the shawl, and now the wind tugs its wisps gently.

Aeson pulls down his underwear shorts with one swift move, kicking them to the ground, and is completely naked. He removes his Khepresh, and his golden Kassiopei mane is contained in a segmented tail.

Dear lord, he looks like a bronzed god.

He stands there confidently, letting me stare at his defined abs and the sculpted V leading to his crotch. My gaze stops and I suck in my breath. His beautiful big dick has started twitching . . . as if my gaze somehow has the tangible power to massage him there, *stroke* him with my very look.

I am not even in the water yet, but there's a wetness and a pulse between my legs.

"Take everything off," he commands me, holding me with his heavy gaze.

Feeling a familiar urgency, I unclasp my bra, releasing my heavy breasts, then pull down my panties and step out of them.

For a moment he freezes, staring at me appreciatively. I recognize his familiar *hunger* in that stare, an intimate thing that he reveals only to *me*.

He then lifts one hand, its gesture beckoning me toward him.

I surge forward and put my hand in his, and he helps me carefully step over the slippery rim into the soothing, delicate water. Then he steps in after me, with a splash.

Here, at the edge, the water barely reaches to our knees. However, the pool floor has a slight incline, so we wade deeper, and it reaches to my waist and slightly below his.

I laugh with pure unbridled joy, and splash my free hand, then sink into the water. Aeson laughs also and sinks with me, supporting me with both hands around my waist.

Ah, this is heaven. . . .

"The water temperature is perfect!" I exclaim.

"It is," he agrees, caressing my upper arms, then leans in to kiss the wildly fluttering pulse point at my neck, pulling me backward. His waterlogged segmented tail tickles against the skin of my shoulders, sending unexpected shivers of pleasure through me.

His mouth sucks powerfully, almost biting my neck, and his lips continue flattening against me, sliding up and down and around my throat and causing me to feel an echo-trail of electricity. A few moments of this, and I twist to face him then wrap my arms around the back of his neck.

Then I move forward, grasping for control, and my own lips fiercely clamp on at the powerful column of his throat, taking a turn at sucking him. We wrestle and splash, bobbing up and down gently in the water, as our bodies start rubbing intimately against each other, skin against skin.

The hard shaft of his penis pushes up at me underwater, poking at my belly. I glance down at it through the transparent water, past my breasts that float before me, protruding from my chest like two inflated balloons.

"Mmm," I moan lightly. In the next instant, Aeson makes a deep sound. Grasping my breasts, he pushes them up and out of the water roughly, then opens his mouth wide around the nipple of one boob and suckles it, pulling my areola flesh deep into his mouth, then repeats with the other. His face is pressed into my chest, roaming from one breast to the other, while I feel the beginning growth of stubble on his jaw scraping my sensitive skin.

The nerve endings in my nipples sing with arousal.

"Please . . ." I whisper desperately. "Aeson, please . . . just put it inside me."

In reply he picks me up by my hips, and the water cascades around me as I'm lifted up. I wrap my legs around him instinctively, almost pressing my belly into his torso, then recalling at the last moment and holding back, so as not to disturb the baby inside.

Splashing, we move closer to the rim of the pool, back into the shallows. At first, I think he is going to sit me down on the stone rim. Then, suddenly, I am flipped over. He turns me around, powerfully but gently. "Put your hands on the stone rim and hold on," he orders, his baritone rumbling near my ear in deep arousal.

I do as I'm told, reaching out with both hands before me to grasp the slightly slippery stone border. He adjusts my body so that I am lying flat on my stomach, semi-floating in the water, knees bent and hips raised.

"Comfortable?" he asks, then slaps my rear lightly with his palms.

"Um-hum," I gasp, moaning, arching my back to push my hips even more toward him. The pulse between my legs is pounding. "Please, *now* . . . just *fu*—"

My words are cut off as his strong hands grasp my hips, positioning me . . . opening my butt-cheeks, fingering my openings . . . and then I feel that first thrust from behind. I suck in air with a shudder as his thick shaft glides inside my vagina, accompanied by an aggressive splash of water. He fills me immediately.

"Ah!" I moan again, as the intense familiar pleasure begins to torment me.

He pulls out, making me moan again. And then he thrusts again, harder, *deeper*, his genitals slapping against my rear.

In seconds, water dances around us.

The rhythm is established. He drives himself into me, over and over, and I wallow like a bit of flotsam pounded by the surf.

I stop feeling the sun, the water. . . .

There is nothing else but the feeling of his *shaft* inside me.

The pressure builds . . . but just before I start to spasm, he bucks hard, then shudders, and comes first.

Ah, my sweet, eager Aeson.

"Argh, sorry . . ." he utters with a groan. "Give me a moment."

"Um-hum," I say, panting, still rotating my hips around his dick, even as he continues to ejaculate. Swirls of his thick, white cum float briefly in the water around us, before dissolving. . . .

About sixty heartbeats later, I feel him stiffening once more, and so I resume grinding against him.

The delicious thrusting recommences. He pounds into me, and this time I orgasm first.

And as my body quiets down, my vision and focus return. I find myself grabbing on to the rim of the pool, still rhythmically rocking in the water (and being rocked by him), but staring with normal awareness at the day glare-drenched surroundings.

Aeson comes again, silently, this time collapsing on my back, wrapping his arms around the front of my torso to keep me from submerging underwater from the kinetic force of his orgasm. Regaining control, he lovingly presses his dripping cheeks and jaw into the back of my neck. His slowing breath tickles me, and then his lips start to kiss my nape. . . .

Then, both of us find ourselves staring at the furry muzzle of a curious wild cat. The big, silky, grey-and-white creature sits only a few feet away on the gravel near the pool, calmly watching us.

CHAPTER 3

"Oh, look! Cat!" I whisper in surprise and delight. The animal is beautiful and graceful, and it has the peaceful innocence of a creature that has never known fear.

"A kitty-cat!" I repeat. "A really big one!"

Aeson's chuckle rumbles against the back of my neck. "A normal-sized one, actually."

"That's right," I continue in the same whisper, still partly breathless, still holding on to the rim of the pool, but now merely floating in the water gently as our bodies have ceased their rhythmic motion. "I often forget how big your domestic cats have evolved to be. Same size as Manala's Khemji."

"That's right," he says, nuzzling the skin of my shoulder, while his large hands still support me lovingly around the waist and rounded belly. Then, his fingers slide up past my baby bump to cup my breasts. He squeezes them, kneading, with that familiar, sensually slow but firm touch, playing with the tips, until my nipples emerge again and harden—at which point I allow a moan to escape.

The cat sits motionless as a post, and stares at us without blinking. Such large golden eyes. . . .

It's been watching us do it . . . is still watching. . . .

"It's feral, right? But not dangerous—or is it? Do you think it's hungry?" I whisper, my voice shuddering on an exhaled breath—and it has nothing to do with fear. Somehow, I'm once again aroused—so much so, that in that moment I hardly care if the puma-sized kitty decides to pounce on my face.

This is the kind of devastating effect Aeson has on me. . . .

"No, not dangerous. Feral has a different meaning in this place. Don't be alarmed, *im vuchusei*," my Imperial Husband says in a deep voice, nibbling at my ear with his teeth. "The cats around the oasis are well fed, well loved . . . and very relaxed, *vuchusei*. Very, *very* relaxed. . . . They know humans mean them no harm."

At the hypnotic sound of his voice, I find myself very, very relaxed indeed, and yet completely tingling with electric awareness. It's as if he is using a *compelling voice* on me.

Holy crap! He is!

"Aeson, you're a sexy asshole!" I exclaim with a stifled laugh.

"Why, is it working?" He laughs in that bottomless-low, mesmerizing voice, then pinches my right nipple lightly, so that I exclaim again, then slap his arm. "That almost hurt!"

"Sorry," he says wickedly. "That was for the asshole."

"Well, you *are!*"

More rumbling soft laughter in my ear. "Sh-sh-sh. . . . You don't want to scare the kitty."

"No, I don't. But it's watching us. And I mean really, *really* watching. A little unsettling, don't you think?"

"Almost as if it's never seen humans *varqood* before." He splashes at me playfully with one hand. "This is a perfect place for such intimate . . . activity. Just imagine: it must've seen hundreds of *varqood* acts in these obscenely sweet pools. Everyone comes here to mate. People and wild creatures."

"Including us. . . ." I smile languidly, glancing at him over my shoulder.

"That's right." He smiles back, and for a few heartbeats we're lost in each other's gazes.

Then I turn completely around, splashing in place awkwardly, so that we're facing each other. I lift my arms around his neck and pull him in for a kiss. The feel of his lips against mine is like homecoming. It starts out soft and sweet, then deepens.

Once more, my pulse picks up the pace, racing in my temples. Soon, my heart is pounding wildly against my ribcage, as though it wants to escape my chest. My breathing shortens, becomes erratic as I kiss him fiercely, in between desperate moans, mouth wide open, grasping for more proximity, for more of *him*.

He responds, his mouth taking over, opening over mine, wrestling, crushing. Our tongues push and yield, and we struggle and share air between us. At some point, as I bounce and shift my floating position in the water, I slip and end up bumping against the rim of the pool with my shoulder.

"Ouch," I whisper, breaking away momentarily. "Sorry, that was me. . . ."

At once he stops and reaches gently to check my shoulder and back of my neck. "Are you okay?"

"Oh yeah, don't worry, I'm fine," I say warmly. "Just got a little too close to the edge . . . that stone."

"That's enough then, let's get out of the water and take a break," Aeson says. "I think it's time for a picnic."

"Okay," I mumble with a silly smile. "But let's try to not scare the kitty?"

"Too late," Aeson says, wrapping his arms around me. And suddenly I'm being lifted out of the water and over the rim of the pool, dripping water everywhere.

At our abrupt motion, the cat comes alive and immediately

springs backward. Moving as fast as a tightly wound coil, it ends up many feet away. However, it's not entirely gone because I see it peeking from around the corner stone of an aqueduct section of a different pond.

"Aww, we scared it," I say with regret, as he sets me down on my own two feet. After floating for so long, I stand of my own accord, but I'm a bit wobbly. And now I feel the scalding-hot, bone-dry desert wind bathe over my naked body. It's a not-so-pleasant contrast after all that nice, cool water, and I feel a strange dizzy sensation, just for a moment. Quickly, I grab hold of Aeson's strong bicep to steady myself. Chalk it up to being pregnant.

Our discarded underclothing is scattered nearby, while the rest of our clothes are stacked on the rim of the pool. The backpack with our supplies sits on the ground just next to it.

Aeson and I don't bother to clothe ourselves. Instead, we pick up our stuff and head in a slightly different direction where a raised section of aqueduct forms three interesting tiers and also creates a minimal amount of shade. There is no grass on the ground, only micro-dunes of sand piled up by the wind to drown some low shrubbery, growing on an incline.

"Here's a nice spot," Aeson says, opening the pack and taking out a large blanket. He spreads it over the sandy incline, and we plop down right on top. The silk of the blanket feels buttery soft and delightful against my bare skin.

"Food!" I say after a few instants, feeling my stomach rumble. *The baby and I are both hungry. . . .* "Let's see what they packed for us." And I dig into the cooler section which keeps our meal items.

I find the bottle of *qvaali*, which must be a thermos because its contents are perfectly ice-cold after all this time in Hel's crazy sunshine. I pour us the fizzy drink into two lightweight glasses.

Aeson and I drink deeply (as always, when I drink *qvaali*, I find myself tasting the faint echo of apple and berry and hops) and then we open the food containers. Multiple savory aromas come wafting from them as soon as I remove the lids. I see sandwich-like wraps, dumplings, sauce, spicy *cheburi* pie pockets dripping with juices, all kinds of delicious pastry tidbits arranged on flat travel plates that require only the lids to be lifted.

We dig in. I stuff my face like a baby vulture, while Aeson eats with somewhat less fury and watches me with fond amusement.

And then he points behind me.

I pause chewing, turn around, and see that the cat is back. It is less than ten feet away, sitting and watching us eat.

"Kitty!" I whisper with delight. "Aeson, it must've smelled our food! Is there anything here that we can feed it? Cats are carnivores, and this is all plant-based."

"Well, no, we don't have any *uzhuut* with us."

"What's *uzhuut*?" I ask.

"That's the specially formulated protein that genetically mimics meat and goes into commercial cat food and other carnivore animal feed." He thinks. "And those spices and seasonings in our dishes will probably make it sick."

"Oh, bummer." I frown slightly. "Is there nothing? Nothing at all here?"

Aeson watches me then slowly lifts one brow. "Maybe some of that *eos* pie crust would work. . . . Though, you can be sure the cat knows how to hunt for itself and has survived just fine so far."

I glance back at the big silvery kitty and see it licking its lips —right in that moment. *Ooh, little pink tongue!*

"Oh, Aeson," I say. "Just because it has *survived* doesn't mean it's not hungry now."

"True." My utterly beloved husband nods with understanding. He then reaches in our food pack and finds the plate with the *eos* pies. Picking out the kind with the blandest, creamy-custard-like filling, he breaks it in half and starts to get up.

As if sensing what's about to happen, the cat leans forward. Stretching its neck, muzzle turned to us, and tail slightly twitching, it takes a slow, careful step in our direction.

Aeson stands on the blanket, muscular and naked, and I observe his tight rear, inches from my face.

"Wait, careful!" I exclaim. "Aeson, put your pants on!"

He pauses, then turns partially, looking down at me. "Huh?"

Now his glorious crotch is in profile, and I look at *him*, all eight inches or more, right there, hanging out at me.

"I said, put your pants on!" I repeat, this time loudly. "Cats like to play with—with dangly bits, and your *big boy* and the—um—two *crown princes* are dangling right out there! What if it jumps up and attacks—"

"My *what?* What did you say?" Aeson's mouth parts and he starts to laugh. "Did you just call my—"

"Yes, your *varqooi*," I say, starting to turn red, for some inexplicable reason, and then widen my eyes and put one hand over my mouth.

"Big boy?" he echoes, his laugh rumbling. "You—you have an actual name for it?"

"Well, not exactly a name, but I do, sort of, think of it like—like—"

"So, you think about my *varqooi?*"

"Oh, holy crap on a stick!" I interrupt, and slap his buttock, my own fierce blush raging. "Pants, first! Cat, second!"

Aeson shakes his head, almost in amazement, still chuckling. "By the time I get dressed, the cat will run off. So, instead—"

He turns around, steps in the direction of the cat and suddenly tosses the *eos* pie, aiming it with perfect precision to land at the kitty's feet.

At once, the cat sniffs, then grabs the pastry in its teeth and takes off running. In an instant it has disappeared among the aqueducts.

Aeson wipes the crumbs off his hands. "Problem solved. And my privates remain intact."

He then sits back down next to me on the blanket, and slowly leans backward to lie against the incline of the ground underneath us. He stretches his gorgeous muscular arms then puts his hands behind his head. With a shadow smile, my Imperial Husband watches me.

I stare back at him, smiling also, then growing serious, mesmerized at his beauty, at his lapis lazuli eyes, narrowed sensually, shaded by the dark lashes. . . . Inevitably, I am compelled to move closer to *im amrevu*. Gently I reach out to touch the soft wisps of his dampened golden Kassiopei hair, carelessly escaping the segmented tail.

And then I lie down with my head against his hard, bronzed chest, listening to his strong heartbeat. He brings one hand gently to caress the back of my neck, fingers running through my messy bun, dislodging it completely so that my long hair is freed.

The desert wind whips it with each fiery gust, even here in the relative shade. . . .

I bury my face in Aeson's chest, and kiss his skin, smelling the faint musky scent that is unique to *him*. He continues lying back, breathing deeply, and his fingers play with my hair.

Moments pass like temple bells . . . perfect peace and silence. This place has a sanctity about it.

We breathe and listen to the wind, and my lips continue to nuzzle his skin.

At some point, I lift up on my elbows and look down at him. I use my hands like feathers to stroke and outline the valleys of his abdomen, making him tense up until his muscles twitch. Then I slide my face further down, moving to the V-shape of his crotch, and I take his big dick in my mouth.

I swallow him as deeply as I can—even as he grows and swells against the back of my throat, even as my husband shudders, throwing his head back, while a gasp of surprise escapes him.

And then I suck him fiercely, until the shaft of the Imperial serpent is as hard as the aqueduct stones in the ruins around us . . . and the head of the serpent becomes the Spring of Anun-Xaat.

CHAPTER 4

I t's hard to tell how much time has passed, but I believe we've napped for at least an hour, maybe two, judging by the shifting, shrinking shadows around the ruins and sparse shrubbery, and the angle of Hel's fierce light as it climbs up higher, approaching zenith.

I open one eye, shifting myself languidly around Aeson's chest, blinking at the desert radiance. He's still asleep, head turned sideways, tendrils of his long golden Kassiopei hair now in a messy segmented tail, stirred by the breeze. I listen to his softly audible breathing, and watch his innocently parted lips with a secret smile on my own. . . .

I really wore him out with my mouth, didn't I? Making him come, over and over, literally *draining* him, and now he's basically passed out with sweet, after-sex relaxation.

Now I snuggle against him, my head lying against his chest. Stirring carefully, without waking him up (though, he's a heavy sleeper and will not wake up easily—something I know well, after sharing his bed all these months), I continue to smile to myself, thinking about how I pleasured him. . . . And how my face is all sticky with his salty *juices*, and so is his crotch—and now, his abdomen and chest, where I've been kissing him afterwards.

Ah, my sweet, insatiable Aeson. . . .

I trail the fingers of one hand lazily to brush against my own lips and feel the sticky semen residue drying at the corners of my mouth. All right, that was epic. And now both of us are a crusty mess. Good thing there are all these water reservoirs and aqueducts around us where we can bathe before moving on.

It's also a good thing, it occurs to me, *that I can wear him out with oral sex and take a small break for myself . . . from him plowing me so often.* Yes, generally speaking, I crave him non-stop. However, being pregnant, I also get tired more easily. And after this morning's hike, and after our lengthy romp in the pool earlier, I'm still exhausted.

Aeson wakes up just then, with a deep shuddering intake of breath, and shifts under me. He groans lightly, which then becomes a deep yawn, stretching his arms, then closes his arms around me in an almost crushing embrace before recalling himself.

"Oh, sorry! Gwen, I didn't squeeze you too much? The baby?"

"Oh, for heaven's sake," I say, with mocking annoyance, lifting my head to stare at him. "You didn't do anything. Please, feel free to crush me some more in your sexy arms." And then I put my own arms around him and stroke the back of his neck and his shoulders.

"Had a good sleep, My Sovereign Lord?" I smile.

"Uh-hum. . . . The best. It's good to get away from all the Imperial obligations—no matter how briefly—and simply be with *you*." He stretches again, glances briefly at his wrist comm unit (which I've forced him to turn off and ignore for the duration of our outing), then sits up, gently displacing me from his chest. "Keep resting—I'll be right back. I need to empty my bladder and water some rather fortunate shrubbery, right over there."

He scrambles up, and I watch his lean, muscular beauty and nakedness with a lazy smile, and then say, "You mean there's still enough liquid left in you, after all those times you—"

"Keep talking like that and I will show you how much *liquid* remains in this body, Imperial Wife." He smiles at me with a searing gaze full of erotic promise. And then he heads to take a leak in a copse of scraggly bushes and desert shrubs not too far from where we are. I watch him standing with his back to me, his body that of a bronzed god, his long golden hair tumbling out of his segmented tail and trailing down his powerful back.

When he returns, I reach for a second thermos bottle in our picnic supplies. This one has ice-cold *nikkari* juice, packed just for me. I pour some in our travel glasses, and Aeson and I both drink with eagerness, quenching our thirst.

"Are we almost out of drinks?" I ask, swirling the bottle to check the contents. "Any more *qvaali* left?"

"All gone," he says, lifting the empty first thermos.

I look around us. "Can we drink the water that's in the aqueducts?"

"Absolutely. It's clean freshwater," he replies. "This close to the source, it is safe to drink, with no filtration necessary. Just make sure it's moving fast, not a still pond. We'll refill the bottles."

"Great," I say, raising my glass. "Then we can safely finish these off."

Aeson turns his head slightly, and cranes his neck, watching me drink and accidentally dribble some of the green *nikkari* juice down my chin, and all over my naked boobs. I can see the way his focus intensifies at once, and the inevitable direction of his gaze.

"Or you can finish *me* off . . . again," he says with a wicked smile.

I just shake my head and smile back, wiping *nikkari* juice from my chin . . . where it's now mingling with the dried Imperial *juices*.

Yeah, his cum is still all over me. . . .

"Aeson," I say. "You're lucky I'm too tired now to do anything but nap and eat. Or I would insist that you get your face down here and give me my own turn."

"I'm happy to oblige." He raises one brow meaningfully and then leans closer to me. "Want me to feast on you, *im vuchusei?*"

"Later," I say with a snort. "Right now, I want to feast on some more dumplings and those savory wraps. Please, pass the dipping sauce."

WE SPEND the next half hour finishing up our picnic items. To be honest, I consume most of it, and Aeson insists I do. Then we refill our drinking bottles from the aqueducts.

Finally, we get back inside the nearest pool and wash off the lovemaking residue, so that we can get dressed again.

Aeson lifts me physically out of the pool, insisting that it's safer that way or I might slip on my own. And then we put on our light clothing to protect us from Hel's radiance and head back through the meandering ruins.

It's definitely after Noon Ghost Time.

At some point, I look around and notice a fast streak of movement near one pool's stone rim. I recognize the same cat, grey and white, not too far from us.

It's following us!

"The kitty is back," I say softly, sliding my fingers over Aeson's bicep.

"I know," he says in amusement. "Once you feed them, it's inevitable."

We walk some more, and I keep glancing around. Sure enough, the cat follows, at a short distance.

"Do we have any more of that creamy-flavored *eos* pie left?" I ask, tugging Aeson's sleeve anxiously.

He pauses to think, then opens up the backpack he's been carrying. I rummage inside, and locate the food containers, most of them now empty. Fortunately, there are a couple of those *eos* pies remaining. I take them out, and break one in half. Then I take a few steps in the direction of the cat, so as not to frighten it.

"Here, kitty, kitty," I whisper gently, leaning forward and offering the piece of pie. "Here, kitty, kitty!"

The cat—in the grand tradition of any other self-respecting feline on any planet—does absolutely nothing in response to my call. It stands watching me, with the tip of its tail barely moving.

So, I toss the piece of *eos* pie its way.

The pie lands several feet short of my goal.

The cat stares with fascination at it, but does not move any closer.

"Go on, kitty!" I say. "I know you want it! Here, I'll back away." And then I retreat a few steps toward Aeson.

The kitty takes a short step forward. And then it seems to have made a decision and approaches the *eos* pie. This time it does not run away but starts eating it right there, looking up occasionally at us, only somewhat wary.

Aeson and I stand watching in amusement. The cat is done eating and, after sniffing the ground and the immediate surrounding area, it gives us a look full of expectation.

I know that look. On Earth, it inevitably means: *Feed me, human.* Apparently, on Atlantis, it means the same thing.

"You want more?" I say, then glance at Aeson with minor regret. "This is all that's left." And I break up the remainder of the *eos* pie in smaller pieces and toss it to the cat. All the while I start carefully approaching it, one short tiptoe step at a time.

Aeson holds back a smile as he watches me move "catlike" toward the cat. I glance at him and note his familiar mannerism, those perfectly controlled lips, and can almost see the warmth and humor in his eyes even though they're hidden behind the blackout sunshades.

Good thing the cat is intensely occupied with sniffing the ground and picking up the little pieces. It gives me just a few wary looks this time as it picks up even the smallest bits and consumes them.

I'm only about five feet away, having crept forward. At this short distance I get a better look at the kitty and notice its fur and markings. It is not pure silver gray, but apparently there is a white collar and chin, plus a white patch leading to its belly. Meanwhile the back is faintly striped with striated beautiful patterns of silver and white.

The creature looks lean and muscular, and its fur is well-groomed, with no signs of mange or any other skin disease. It appears healthy and definitely not malnourished, though it seems a little young. . . . Of course, I can't be entirely sure, not with these oversized Atlantean cats, but I have this gut feeling that it's not entirely fully grown.

I lean forward and take another step, slowly reaching out with my hand. The cat sniffs the air in my direction, its head stretching toward me. Then, as though recalling the situation, it gives a little hiss, and jumps backward. And in seconds it's gone, disappearing once again in the surrounding maze of waterways and shrubbery.

"Awww," I say, standing up and looking at Aeson with regret. "It's such a cute and pretty kitty. I really wanted to pet it."

"Well, it is a wild little thing. It got a nice meal from you, so now it probably ran away to hide and digest it," Aeson says to make me feel better.

"Little thing? You call that a *little* thing?" I say with a laugh.

"It's still young," he replies, not bothering to hide his amusement. And then we continue walking.

• • •

"HOW ARE YOU FEELING?" Aeson asks me with concern a few minutes later, seeing that my pace has slowed down somewhat. "Do you need to rest?"

"I'm okay," I say with a faint smile and a tired wave of my hand.

"Are you sure?" He stops, then puts his hand on my skin to feel my forehead and neck. "You seem a little overheated. All right, that's enough. Let me call a shuttle from the *depet* so that you don't need to walk the rest of the way—"

"*Oh, no!*" I exclaim in a hurry, throwing out my hand to point around us. "We're almost there, and I wouldn't want to miss a moment in this amazing place. I'm fine!"

"At least let's get you a wet cloth so that you can wipe down your face and neck to cool yourself. Meanwhile, you need to drink from your water bottle!"

He sets the pack down and removes a small towel, then goes to dip it in the nearest running water reservoir. While he does that, I pick up a water bottle from the pack and take deep gulps of the cool liquid.

Aeson hands me the wet towel and I use it to wipe my neck area, which brings immediate relief in the scalding hot wind.

I look out in the distance where I see a long oval object hovering low over the horizon, silhouetted against the fiery sky and nearby ruins. It's our luxury *nubu depet*, parked in the air.

"See, there's our boat." I point. "We're very close now. We'll be there in ten daydreams."

Aeson nods. "All right—but the moment you feel off, in any way, you tell me. Do you understand?"

"Yes, my Sovereign Lord and Master," I say with a kiss-shaped pout at my Imperial Husband.

"I'm serious, Gwen." He takes off his sunshades so that I can see his eyes and their beautiful lapis-lazuli-blue intensity. "You should not overheat. If you start feeling sick—"

"You're so sweet and fussy and ridiculous," I say, lowering

my bottle, then step toward him and pull him in with one arm for an impulsive kiss.

The moment I bring his head down closer to me and our mouths connect, I feel all my exhaustion evaporating. An electric charge of sensuality rides through me, striking at me from the skin of my lips and throughout my body . . . and his lips press harder against mine.

We kiss, everything forgotten—but, briefly. Because the next instant I'm wrapped in Aeson's arms and lifted physically from the ground.

"What are you doing?" I giggle, surfacing from our kiss.

"I'm going to carry you the rest of the way," he says, his rich baritone voice caressing me, his breath soft at my throat, near my ear.

"Aeson, no, I'm too heavy!" I protest, with my arms wrapped around his neck, my water bottle sloshing, loosely held in my fingers. "Besides, what about the backpack with our stuff?"

"*Varqood* the backpack. I'll have someone come and pick it up. Or it can stay here for some tourist to find."

"You are officially insane." I laugh, helpless in his arms. "Please promise to put me down if you get tired."

APPARENTLY, the Imperator never gets tired, because Aeson carries me in his powerful arms all the way back, for the last portion of our spectacular outing. Soon, we emerge from the Anun-Xaat labyrinth of the waterways into the greater desert, right before the hovering *nubu depet*.

The grand vessel's ramp stands lowered invitingly, waiting for us to board.

Aeson sets me down on my own two feet, just as two uniformed servants emerge to assist us. One of them goes back to retrieve the backpack left somewhere in the ruins—I'm told it has a built-in tracker. The second one informs Aeson with a polite bow that he has an important communication waiting for him from the Deshi capital. Apparently, a formal invitation has arrived from Xois, from none other than the Pharikon of New Deshret.

We head up the gentle incline of the ramp and into the luxurious, cool interior of the vessel. At the top of the ramp, I glance backward at the mauve and silver dunes of the Heruvar desert to take in the spectacular sight one more time. . . .

That's when I see the sliver-grey streak of movement—a sleek feline shape bounding up the ramp right behind us, overtaking us, and conveniently swallowed up in the darkened interior of our ship.

CHAPTER 5

"*Bashtooh! Im amrevu*, we've been adopted." Aeson takes off his dark sunglasses and starts to laugh.

"Oh no, the cat!" I exclaim at the same time. But I have a goofy expression on my face, and a smile.

I look up at Aeson and notice he has a similar expression, quite rare for him, that of childish joy. The joy flickers briefly, then his lips tighten in a smoothly controlled line (which I realize is for the three solemn-faced staff members inside who stand politely at attention and watch us approach) and he raises one brow at me in a brief signal of mutual understanding.

We step inside the ship's bay, and are greeted by a blast of cool air that acts like heavenly balm after the dry heat of the desert outside. In that moment there's no sign of the cat which has gone ahead of us and disappeared.

"My Imperial Sovereign," one of the uniformed servants asks, "what should be done with the wild animal that just boarded the Imperial *depet*?"

"Nothing," Aeson replies. "It's coming with us."

"Yes, please!" I exclaim. "Please don't hurt it!"

"Of course, my Sovereign Lady."

"Find it at some point—gently—and see if you can provide it with some species-appropriate protein and water." Aeson adds. "It's a cat, apparently a young feral one. Try not to get scratched. And keep me informed."

"Very well, Imperial Sovereign." The servant nods, lowering his head, but I notice a quickly hidden smile on the face of a different servant next to him. I can only imagine the "fun" the staff will have, trying to catch and isolate the cat inside the huge luxury *depet*.

"The Imperatris and I will have some refreshments in our quarters now," Aeson says to a different servant. "Meanwhile, set course to Xois. You may take off at once."

And we proceed upstairs to our private deck.

"I WONDER where the kitty is now?" I keep saying, as we relax in our spacious suite with grand windows offering a spectacular view of the desert and the Heruvar cityscape— silvery mauve, lavender-grey, with shards of reflected light— floating past us outside, while the kitchen staff serves us a late *dea* meal. "Did they catch it? Is it okay?"

"No news yet," Aeson replies.

"I bet it's found some impossible, tiny spot to hide," I muse with a smile, taking a large bite of aromatic noodles. "Probably stuffed itself under furniture or curled up in some box—or—"

"Sleeping in catlike fashion, no doubt," my husband replies, then checks his wrist unit.

"Is that the message from the Pharikon?" I try to peek at the holographic display above his wrist.

Aeson doesn't look up, engrossed. "Yes. We're being sent the details of the invitation and the event itself. Deshi court protocol is just as particular as *Atlantida's*."

"Oh no!" I say. "Do we have to make an appearance at their

court? I'd rather not be seen by a bunch of stuffy nobles when I'm bloated like a whale—"

"You're not bloated like a whale," Aeson replies, glancing up in amusement. "You're glowing."

"I'm glowing like a bloated, radioactive jellyfish from the ocean depths that swallowed a whale!" I exclaim with my mouth full of noodles, trying not to spit with laughter and choke at the same time.

Aeson just wiggles one brow at me. It's amazing how much he can communicate with those handsome, raven-black brows of his—so black that they have a slight bluish tint. . . .

"You'll be pleased to know that it will be a small gathering, and Crown Princess Sheolaat will be in attendance," he says, continuing to read the holo-message on his wrist. "I, meanwhile, will be pleased to have my heart brother Rumeiar there."

"Oh. . . ." I grow serious, feeling a sudden sharp pang of memories. "Princess Sheolaat. . . . I haven't seen her since—since the alien war . . . and our Coronation. And only very briefly, that day. I'd love to speak a bit longer with her."

"You'll certainly have the chance tonight. As soon as we finish moving scenically over Heruvar—I don't want you to miss the beautiful modern rooftop view of their city—I'll have the *depet* go straight up into orbit and take a shortcut, then make its drop directly over Xois. We'll be there in about two hours. Most of those two hours will be taken up by this slow scenic sailing part, over Heruvar."

I nod appreciatively. "I'm loving this view. So much crystalline glasswork in the upper tiers of these skyscrapers. Makes me think a little of Dubai or Abu Dhabi on Earth, with their gorgeous modern buildings."

WE CONTINUE NIBBLING on our *dea* meal leisurely and watching the serene, slow grandeur unrolling before us, a coral reef of gilded roofs, geodesic domes, and other landmarks sparkling in the light of Hel. Sections of greenery with lush parks are interspersed with busy urban and suburban sprawl. We're sailing high over normal city traffic hover lanes, so our path and view is unhindered by other vehicles. Aeson tells me that *nubu depets* of this size are considered heavy aircraft, hence not suitable for city-level air traffic. In addition, we are a foreign vessel, so it would be inappropriate to venture lower without specific clearance.

Eventually we pass out of the city and into the encroaching desert, where occasional settlements and structures are scattered like tiny distant shrubs in the dunes, and only a few long, dark veins of roads cut through the barren ground.

Time to shoot straight up into orbit.

And we do.

I'm used to it by now. No need to strap in with seatbelts, no need to do anything but relax and enjoy the smooth sailing in this incredible ship. Even the panoramic windows remain uncovered, exposed directly to space, to give us an actual, non-holographic, spectacular view of the layers of atmosphere turning dark blue, then pitch black, as we rise.

We emerge into cosmic orbital night, and see the sharp, incandescent disk of Hel sweep past our view in all its blinding glory, despite the shielded, super reinforced glass alloy of the view port windows. We also see the curvature of the planet Atlantis, and then we turn, and the *depet* streaks forward at an incredible speed then plummets back down again in a matter of a few daydreams. I never cease to wonder how the G-forces barely affect this luxury ship, so well and safely it is cocooned in its plasma shield.

And then we fall back down through the atmosphere, into the light, and the early teal sunset, to Xois.

· · ·

WE ARRIVE three hours before our formal evening event which is scheduled for eighth hour of Ra. It gives us plenty of time to relax and prepare.

We're in the final days of the month of Yellow Ghost Moon, which on Imperial *Atlantida* would indicate the end of autumnal Yellow Season and the cooling days of approaching winter. Here, however—on the opposite side of the planet, the Lower Hemisphere—it is the end of spring in New Deshret, heading into fierce summer and high heat. Fortunately, unlike landlocked desert Heruvar, Xois is a coastal metropolis. The magnificent capital is located on the shore of the Gulf of Eos, just as Poseidon is located on the Golden Bay. The weather is much cooler here, pleasant and perfect at this time of year, according to Aeson. Plus, they've got their weather tech under control after all the malfunctioning earlier in the year.

As Honored Guests of the Pharikon, we arrive directly at the Deshi Palace and our Imperial *nubu depet* parks itself in a huge airfield, twice as large as that of the Imperial Palace in Poseidon.

"They built and expanded this airfield much later than our *Atlantida* counterpart," Aeson tells me as we come down the ramp and into a considerably cooler city, this time accompanied by his usual Imperial guards and mine, and numerous servants carrying our luggage.

Several formal-looking officials and three hovercars stand hover-parked nearby, waiting to take us directly to the Palace buildings that loom in the distance. The driver of the first car approaches, and I see a vaguely familiar, tall, and lean man dressed in stylish fashion. He has a copper-red cast to his skin, and wears a blue armband. Seeing Aeson, his serious face transforms with a slow smile. And then he gives a very familiar military salute of the Star Pilot Corps.

"Imperial Sovereign—Command Pilot—*daimon*. Welcome to Xois, Kass!" says the man, and without any further ceremony he steps forward.

"Rumeiar!" Aeson says loudly, his own face breaking out into a smile. "Good to see you, *daimon!*"

"I almost called you Commander, out of old habit," Rumeiar says to Aeson.

"Yes, well, I don't think SPC Fleet Commander Keigeri would appreciate that," Aeson almost snarfs, then recovers himself, since we are in public, and there are Imperial guards, and Deshi officials present.

Aeson has grown somewhat lax in his formal Imperial Protocol, it occurs to me. *Is it my fault? Must be my bad influence.* Maybe he just doesn't care as much about the formalities anymore, having become so much more relaxed as the Imperial Sovereign.

Or maybe it's that I've drained him sexually, just a few hours ago. Yes, he's very, very *relaxed today. . . .*

I hold back a naughty smile. Then, forcing myself not to dwell on our vigorous intimate activities of the morning in this less-than-appropriate moment, I recall how, as a newly minted head of state, Aeson had to resign his position as SPC Commander.

It would've been a conflict of interest to be the chief commanding officer of the international Star Pilot Corps *and* the Archaeon Imperator of *Atlantida* at the same time. So, immediately after his Coronation, Aeson appointed Pilot Oalla Keigeri to take his place as the head of the SPC. Keruvat apparently declined, in favor of his love, and Erita had no interest in High Command whatsoever. In fact, Aeson told me, Erita has informed him repeatedly that she is perfectly happy to be a Command Pilot permanently, and who wants all that stress and bureaucracy of being Fleet Commander?

Meanwhile, in the here and now, Rumeiar chuckles. "Appreciate such a blunder? No, she would not." Then he glances warmly at me. "Sovereign Lady Gwen, welcome!"

"Gwen, this is Rumeiar Heru, fellow *astra daimon* and heart brother," Aeson says, turning to me. I believe you never actually met him during the whirlwind events of the Coronation. He was in our Honor Guard."

"I know I've *seen* you then, but we just haven't spoken formally, that's right," I say with enthusiasm. "So nice to meet you!" Stepping forward, I offer my hand to Rumeiar in a simple Earth gesture.

Oh crap! In all this lax casualness, I've forgotten that royals don't shake hands or touch anyone under formal circumstances, and I'm the Imperatris of frigging *Atlantida.* . . .

Before I take my hand back, Rumeiar meets it with his own in an equally simple gesture. We shake, and Rumeiar apparently is familiar with this Earth greeting, because his grasp is well practiced, basic and warm.

"The honor and pleasure are all mine," he says to me. "And now, allow me to drive you to the Palace, because it might be the only casual time I'll get to spend with Kass, before the inevitable formalities take over."

We get in the hovercar, which basically saves us the trouble of walking across a very long stretch of open pavement (and in my current condition, I appreciate it), while our Imperial guards and staff get in the vehicles behind us.

Once seated inside next to Aeson, I glance out of the tinted, impermeable security window on my side and briefly observe Tuar Momet, my personal chief bodyguard, watch our surroundings like a hawk and exchange glances with Aeson's chief guard, before disappearing inside the second vehicle.

Aeson and Rumeiar speak with humor, exchange SPC gossip, and make a few *astra daimon* in-jokes while we speed across the airfield. In moments, we arrive at the gates leading into a sprawling, cultured park, very similar in structure to the one in *Atlantida* surrounding the Imperial Palace. Once again, it's as if New Deshret is attempting to outdo the splendor of Imperial *Atlantida*. Everything here seems just a little bigger, bolder, including the immense complex of buildings that include the main Palace structure.

We part ways with Rumeiar (we'll be seeing him again later tonight) and enter the Pharikon Palace, first ascending a long series of marble stairs which lead directly into an immense hall with a grand cupola ceiling. Walking up these steep stairs, I find that I must hold Acson's hand. . . .

Here, rows of uniformed servants line up before us, and we are immediately conducted to our Guest Quarters via a swift elevator. Technically, we could've stayed on board our *nubu depet*, gotten formally dressed there in our own luxury bedroom, and simply arrived in time for the Court Event in our full Imperial Regalia. But that wouldn't have been the correct Protocol.

So now we have to bring our formal clothing and other required things with us and get dressed in the Guest Quarters where we will later be staying for the night, so as not to offend the Royal Deshi hospitality.

As soon as we arrive in the huge and splendid guest suite, and are left alone at last, I let out my breath in exhaustion and turn to the Archaeon Imperator of *Atlantida*, my beloved.

"Aeson," I say. "I think . . . I seriously need a nap. Like, *now*. I'm about to pass out."

My Imperial Husband simply reaches for me and sweeps me up in his arms. He lifts and carries me across the ornately decorated bedchamber to a grand bed worthy of our own immense bed in the Imperator's Quarters back home. He lays me gently down on top of the satin-soft coverlet, and I sink in a sea of softness, with a mountain of pillows behind me.

"Sleep," he says in his deep, low baritone, commanding me —and judging by the serpentine, honeyed tone, possibly *compelling* me—while standing over me like my own golden god. And then he leans down and presses his lips gently against my forehead.

"Sleep, *im amrevu* . . ." he repeats in a whisper, resting his arms on both sides of me, and I close my eyes, sensing his warm, strong presence all around me.

THE NEXT TIME I open my eyes, shuddering awake, emerging out of the most delicious sleep, I see deep twilight in the grand windows. Several light orbs have bloomed into being, filling the delicate cream and gold décor of the chamber with an enhanced amber glow. Aeson is sitting at a small desk nearby, staring at a small monitor full of text and moving images. I suppose he has to catch up with work at some point during our intimate journey.

"Oh!" I moan, yawning deeply. "How long was I out? What time is it? I hope I didn't oversleep."

Aeson turns toward me with a comfortable look. "You didn't. No rush, we still have about two hours. Did you sleep well?"

"Uh-huh," I say and yawn again, then pat the coverlet next to me. "Come here, mister. But no, wait . . . I need to pee."

He chuckles and points to the bathroom suite, as I scoot over on the bed then haul myself upright. I find the bathroom with its truly throne-like gilded toilet, use it, then splash my face over the carved basin of the fountain sink.

I glance around this opulent place and see flowers everywhere, together with a vast array of expensive toiletries. Deshi lotions, oils, and cosmetics in crystal bottles line the chamber, along with billowing stacks of towels. Meanwhile, a great sunken tub stands in the center, and not one but three showers with various shining metal fixtures are built into niches in the walls. I'll be taking a nice long shower in a few minutes, to get ready for my Imperial outfit, but first. . . .

I return to the bedroom, feeling very well rested after my hour-long nap, and slightly breathless with anticipation. I'm still wearing the light dress I've had on since the *nubu depet* when I changed into it right after our visit to the ruins of Anun-Xaat. Underneath, I have my usual support bra on for decency (mostly to reduce boob swing in public), but I'm not wearing any panties. And . . . it must be my hormones, because I suddenly feel. . . .

"Aeson," I say in a soft voice. "Come here."

He turns around once more, and then sees the look in my eyes, the expression of *need*.

Ah, he knows that expression of mine so well. . . . He freezes, then slowly stands up.

My Imperial Husband approaches me in two strides, and already his shirt is coming off. Then, he undoes the clasp of his pants. I start grabbing and pulling at his waist in a poor attempt to help him but, in my urgency, I think I only make matters worse since I'm not that great with Atlantean clasps and buttons. . . .

"Please, hurry," I say, hitching my dress up over my waist, revealing my big belly and my privates.

His breathing starts coming loudly and he is completely naked before me, his cock already hard and rising.

I fall backward on the big, squishy-soft bed, and part my legs for him, spreading wide. A wild pulse is pounding down there, and I am soaking wet. . . .

Aeson falls on the bed next to me, but then immediately pulls me up, and positions me above him, caressing the inside of my thighs, leaving me straddling his abdomen in our usual safe, pregnancy position. I wrap my arms around his strong neck, grasp his shoulders and hold on. As we move and adjust ourselves, the shaft of his cock unintentionally slides and pokes against that engorged little button just above the opening of my vagina, sending a sharp pang of angry urgency through me.

Rub me . . . fuck me. . . .

He inserts fingers inside me to make sure I'm ready, and when I pant and moan at his touch, he *knows*.

"Fuck," I cry out, this time out loud. "Just *fuck* me, please! No, wait, let me—"

Fiercely I grab his big cock and push it inside me, impaling myself up to his balls. Ah, the sweet overwhelming pain-pleasure!

Aeson makes a deep corresponding sound, and then we begin our rhythmic struggle—glide and pump, in and out, slick with my juices. . . . My dress still covers my upper body, but I'm too much in the moment, bouncing up and down on his shaft, moaning wildly, absolutely out of control, until suddenly I come, quick and violent.

The rocking currents sweep throughout me while I continue to spasm around him, over and over, caught up in a multiple cascade of waves. And in that same moment I hear his harsh breathing stop . . . then the deep, male groan erupts as he comes too, hard and hot, gushing inside me. My vaginal muscles contract around him, and we ride together, his strong hands squeezing and pinching the globes of my hips.

The tidal wave recedes, and eventually we grow still, collapsed in one pile of sweaty limbs.

"*Varqood* . . . Gwen. . . . Ah!" Aeson says, looking up at me with an expression of relaxed bliss. It's such an ephemeral expression, one which I so love to see in him. "That was better than good. Unfortunately, we need to get ready for Court."

"Oh, no," I moan. "Screw it."

But my husband pinches my behind again, wickedly, and his eyes gleam with promise. "Don't worry, I'll make it up to you *afterwards* . . . much later, tonight. Over and over, I'll screw *you*."

CHAPTER 6

The Pharikon of New Deshret sends a whole cadre of servants to attend to us as we prepare for the evening reception with our royal host. As the Imperator and Imperatris of *Atlantida* we already have our own servants with us, so it becomes a very crowded suite, and some of the Deshi staff gets sent back with polite and profuse thanks.

Aeson and I bathe and shower separately, then are assisted by our personal staff, as we put on our chosen outfits that we've brought with us from the *depet*. I put on a gorgeous long dress of green fabric of various iridescent shades layered one over the other like an onion of gauze and delicate cobwebs. The style is simple and loose—a non-revealing bodice with a high collar around my neck, all of it continuing downward, blending into the skirt portion around my waist and hips. The green layers flow around my enlarged belly in elegant fashion, and cascade to the floor.

My hair is styled into a complex work of art, a sculptured up-do, studded with glittering emeralds and jade droplets and framed by delicate golden netting. I wear matching chandelier earrings with more green gems, and slim bracelets on my wrists.

There's my wedding ring of course, always on my finger—shining a stunning deep blue, with purple and rose highlights. The stone is Pegasus Blood of the rarest color, finely faceted and glittering like a star. . . . I glance at it often, and think of Aeson's larger wedding ring, complementary to mine (sans stone), encircling his own elegant digit.

Finally, I get my High Court cosmetics applied, by two maidservants whom I've chosen for this task because they've "passed" Consul Denu's discriminating criteria—survived his school of Face Art—and have been trained by his personal servant Kem.

Tonight, I wear a deep, earthy-red hue of *noohd* on my lips, an almost brown or sienna shade. And my eyes are outlined in the allure of smoky black and brown kohl.

Aeson wears an elegant formal ink-blue jacket, matching trousers, a pale cream dress shirt, and a wide, gem-studded gold collar around his neck. It's an outfit intended to remind the world of his Blue Court, but also manages to emphasize his wide shoulders, lean and perfectly toned muscular body, and Imperial bearing.

Neither my husband nor I wear crowns for this event. Formal crowns are customarily worn only on our home soil during formal Court Assemblies, and not taken out of the country—such is the ancient custom of Imperial *Atlantida*.

By the time we're done dressing, it is time to go. We mustn't be late, for that would be impolite to our hosts.

"Ready, *im amrevu?*" Aeson takes my hand and meanwhile stares at me with a very familiar, complex, serpentine intensity, never blinking . . . as if I were a feast.

"Yes, My Sovereign Lord." I look up at him, unable to hold back a slow smile, because I recognize that look on him, the heightened focus when he is about to use the *compelling voice*, except at this moment it's unwitting and unintentional.

And then he comes out of it, almost self-consciously, blinks as if awakening, and admits out loud, "Gwen . . . ah, I would much rather stay here with you, and—"

"I know," I say, taking his hand and massaging his warm fingers with my own. "But we must go."

And surrounded by Imperial guards, we exit our Guest Quarters and proceed to the reception.

THE ARCHITECTURE around us seems so familiar. Not sure if it is entirely Landing Period original (as far as being destroyed and rebuilt over the centuries), but this Palace, if I recall my lessons correctly, is as ancient as the Imperial Palace in *Atlantida*. Both were built at approximately the same time in true rival fashion. And many of the elements were copied from one to the other.

The Deshi Grand Assembly Hall is not our destination. Instead, a much more intimate venue greets us in the form of a mid-sized chamber with a lofty gilded ceiling decorated with frescoes depicting stylized spiraling clouds and stars. A colonnade of sleek ebony columns of veined, marble-like stone lines the walls on both sides.

In the center stretches a long table set for possibly twenty people. A centerpiece of pale silvery rose flowers arises from the cloth in the middle, and the tall backed chairs are carved of wood and polished with age and elegance.

Orbs of warm golden light float over the table at even intervals casting a steady "paper lantern" glow.

There is a small group of people gathered in the room. Everyone is standing—except for one elderly man in a black robe sparely trimmed in gold, seated in a prominent spot near the table. The Pharikon of New Deshret occupies a comfortable chair that is not quite a throne, with several pillows stuffed around his back and at his elbows, plus a pillowed footrest upon which his feet in fabric slippers are resting. He appears to be napping, or merely relaxing with his eyes closed, while the others in the room talk quietly and politely among themselves.

Areviktet Heru's face is deeply wrinkled, with parchment skin like river red clay, and his long white hair is pulled back and gathered into four segmented tails. He wears a gold circlet around his forehead, which is also not a formal crown, I recall, but more of a designation of high nobility.

Among others in the room, I immediately recognize Crown Princess Sheolaat, a statuesque young woman almost as tall as I am, with skin of a reddish-coppery hue, similar in coloration to Rumeiar who is also present. Sheolaat's black hair is a magnificent long mane, worn loose with nothing but a slim circlet at her forehead, dark eyes, strong and beautiful brows, and a nose with a prominent bridge softened by a rounded face.

She is clad in a long, dark wine-red dress, smart and businesslike, which reveals little of her figure and reaches her throat. Here, in a surprising departure from her otherwise conservative look, a spectacular wide collar encircles her neck. Faceted gems of various shades of red sparkle gorgeously, conjuring the illusion of a ring of fire around her face.

Her expression when she sees us is welcoming, and she turns at once in our direction.

In the same moment, we are formally announced by a booming-voiced head servant at the entrance:

"Aeson Kassiopei, Archaeon Imperator of Imperial *Atlantida* and Gwenevere Kassiopei, Archaeona Imperatris!"

We begin to cross the chamber and the Pharikon's eyes immediately fly open, forming small ebony slits in a sea of wrinkles. At the same time, his face is transformed with a brief smile. He makes a little grunt and barely straightens in his comfy chair. Raising one hand to beckon us casually, he speaks in an energetic but slightly rasping old man's voice in his usual, awkwardly accented English, "There you are, young Imperator and your blessed Wife! *Nefero niktos!* Come, come!"

"*Shiokuh nuuttos*, Pharikon Areviktet Heru," Aeson responds with a comfortable smile of his own. "*Mayvahar eini ulu guvadaat.*"

Thank you for your kind hospitality, in Deshi.

"*Shiokuh nuuttos*, Pharikon," I echo Aeson, saying the only phrase I really know in Deshi.

"*Wixameret!* Welcome!" the Pharikon continues, in *Atlanteo* and English, covering all bases.

And now, with the linguistic formality out of the way, he switches to English, on my behalf. I realize it is a very gracious host gesture, since normally they would simply converse back and forth in Deshi and *Atlanteo*.

Out of nowhere, servants produce two well-cushioned chairs for the two of us, so that we sit oddly, in the middle of the room, facing the Pharikon. As I sit down with a tiny, awkward pause, I glance around at the rest of the courtiers and the Crown Princess. Apparently, they are all to remain on their feet. Deshi customs are indeed odd . . . or maybe it's just the Pharikon's personal quirks and old age at play here.

"So, are you young ones enjoying your Amrevet Days?" Areviktet Heru asks with a little naughty smile, then chuckles.

Aeson starts to smile then laughs, in reply. "Well . . . it's been wonderful indeed, Pharikon. We've been traveling for only one day, but my Wife and I cannot be more pleased." And he glances at me with an unmistakable teasing look.

"Oh, yes," I hurry to say. "It has been an amazing journey so far! And I love what I've seen of your beautiful nation. Heruvar, the desert, the Spring of Anun-Xaat—"

"Yes, yes," the Pharikon interrupts me with a wave of his wrinkled hand. "All that is good, but how is your Husband pleasing you in bed? How you say in your English, 'make love?' 'Make *amrevet*?' Make sure he treats you well and worships you properly as the Mother of your Nation. Better than his own Father treated his Blessed Consort, the lovely

Devora—eh, never mind. . . ." He ends on a grumbling mutter.

At once, Aeson becomes very still and controlled, and his smile recedes.

Oh no! This is a sensitive subject for Aeson. Poor Aeson!

My pulse starts racing with instant agitation on my husband's behalf. I open my mouth to say something, anything, but the Pharikon must've realized he's gone a bit too far, so he clears his throat several times, raspingly, saving me the trouble of an awkward filler comment.

I look up briefly and see Princess Sheolaat watching us and the Pharikon with an expression of compassion as she stands nearby.

Is this a rare moment of age-based loss of mental acuity on the old man's part? I wonder with sadness. For as long as I've known the Pharikon, he's always been so sharp.

"Ah, let's not bring up Romhutat . . . my apologies, Aeson," Areviktet says after a pause, and his narrowed eyes seem a little unfocused by his own slight blunder. "You're the Imperator now, so good, good. How is your Mother?"

"My Mother, the Mag-Imperatris, is as well as can be," Aeson says calmly. He's used the moments to recover himself, but I note that some of the light humor in his expression has been deadened. "She resides with us at the Palace, for which I'm ever glad."

"Good, good," Pharikon Heru nods. "A good son never abandons his blessed Mother. Now, let's eat!" And just as suddenly he motions with one hand to the servants who approach to help him rise out of his chair

So, this is going to be a casual yet surprise-filled, oddball evening, I think, as Aeson and I both rise from our seats also, letting our chairs be taken away.

Two servants assist Areviktet Heru to walk the few paces to the long table, holding him gently by the elbows, until he reaches the center seat. They slide the chair back, and he lowers himself tiredly with a grunt.

The Pharikon really *is* showing his age.

Next, Aeson and I are directed to sit in the chairs directly across from him—not on two distant opposite ends of the length of the table, but on the short side, at a conversational distance. Unlike Protocol-driven Imperial *Atlantida*, there's less seating formality here—or maybe it's just that this is not an official state affair.

As soon as the three of us sit, the rest of the guests take their places around the table. Once again, the order seems to be mostly casual. I don't know any of these people but they are likely distinguished nobility or relatives of the Royal Deshi House. Sheolaat sits next to her elderly royal uncle (and across the short side of the table from me), while Aeson is directly across from the Pharikon. Rumeiar Heru takes the seat on Aeson's other side.

An unfamiliar dark-haired matron in a deep violet dress sits down next to me on the other side, and smiles, saying nothing. Instead, she observes Pharikon Heru settling in his chair, and when he appears to be comfortable, she takes it upon herself to wave with one bejeweled hand to the serving staff.

The servants begin carrying the dishes for the *niktos* meal. At once, a delicious aroma of heat and spices and pungent flavor fills the chamber. Deshi cuisine is not too different from that of Imperial *Atlantida*, with the exception of being even more spicy.

Aeson had warned me about it earlier, suggested I might carefully sample things first before rushing to eat, considering my condition and my less than stable stomach. "Good thing I love spicy food," I told him. "Don't worry about me or my pregnant tummy. All good!"

Aeson merely shook his head with a light smile. "I always will, you know."

Well, now I get to test my ability to handle Deshi spices.

Or maybe not.

The food plate set before me by a solicitous servant is not the same as what is being served to everyone else. I stare at the bowl of creamy liquid topped with crunchy bits and sprigs of leaves and flowers, then compare it to the vibrant fare on other people's plates.

"*Chubre* soup . . ." the matron to my left whispers to me tactfully in somewhat stilted English. "Very good for *baby*."

"Oh. . . ." I glance at her kind but firm expression and decide to accept this form of hospitality. "Thank you."

I pick up my utensil and try the soup. It's definitely on the bland side, but very pleasant, reminiscent of a rich cream-of-mushroom with just a hint of savory tang. And the crunchy bits are some kind of toasted nuts that add a delightful mouth-feel.

"You like?" the matron asks, leaning close to my ear.

"It's delicious, thank you," I reply between soundless, controlled slurps. The soup really is good, and I can probably pick up and drink the whole bowl in an instant and then have another.

Aeson glances at me, with amusement. *I bet he knows*, I think. He knows exactly how ravenous I get these days.

Meanwhile, the conversation around the table picks up. The Pharikon eats silently at first, intent on his own bowl—which, I notice, looks very much like my own soup. But after slurping up most of the soupy contents before him, he looks up and says to Aeson, "Remind me to have a talk with you in private before you leave tonight."

"Ot course." Aeson takes a drink of *raidu* from his tall glass. It's a mildly alcoholic Deshi beverage similar to Earth wine, which the servants also don't serve me. Instead, I get to drink a fruity sparkling thing.

In the meantime, Princess Sheolaat, seated opposite me, speaks up for the first time, in her rich alto. "You are glowing with life, Gwen. Impending motherhood becomes you."

The moment I hear her unforgettable Logos voice, its velvety, bone-deep timbre, I am instantly swept away to the events of the alien war, and our *astroctadra* Helios system planetary alignment mission. I remember her voice raised, along with mine and the others in a great Plural Logos Voice Chorus, as we sing the voice sequences to put up an immense Quantum Containment Shield over the whole Helios system and defeat the trans-dimensional enemy.

And then I recall, with a pang of old agony, the terror of being marooned in space amid the wreckage of the Deshi battle barge that carried me to my alignment coordinates. . . . So many Fleet officers and crew from New Deshret died on that day, supporting *me* and mine, in our joint mission.

Guilt strikes me, hard. . . .

I blink, meeting Sheolaat's friendly gaze. I really do need to respond to her pleasant, conversational small talk.

"Thank you," I respond with a smile and a slightly embarrassed shrug. "We weren't exactly planning on it yet, but, here I am. . . . I blame the crazy circumstances of the past months." And in that moment I wonder about the young woman herself and her own status.

As if reading my mind, she says, "I am unattached as of yet, so none of that for me."

"And that's perfectly okay," I rush to say. "With all the responsibilities before you, there's plenty of time to make life choices regarding a spouse or family. When the time comes, no one says you have to rule with a Consort, right? I mean—apologies if this is—"

"True, there is no such requirement in our laws."

"Okay, good," I say. "Because that would be—*unbearable* if it were."

Sheolaat's eyes brighten with mischief. "Unbearable would be the perfect description for it." And then she skillfully switches to a less sensitive subject. "How is your family, Gwen?

Your brothers, George and Gordie? Your little sister? *Ter* Charles?"

"Oh, they're all just fine," I say. "Thank you so much for asking. My Father, *Ter* Charles, is very busy coordinating research at the various cultural museums, and he's been doing visiting work here too, at a number of Deshi sites. George is still undecided, but trying out different career options. Gracie is thriving in the Fleet, and Gordie just had a promotion at his place of work."

"Please give all of them my regards," the Princess says. "And tell *Ter* Charles the next time he is in Xois, to contact me."

"I will." I smile, looking into her dark, earnest eyes. "And how is your little brother, Keigo?"

Sheolaat raises one brow. "The little—how do you say in English—antelope? Yes, he gallops all around the house, making our mother crazy, but otherwise all is well. Soon he will be old enough to relieve his poor tutors and attend proper Cadet school."

"Here, in Xois?" I ask, recalling that New Deshret has their own equivalent of Fleet Cadet School.

Sheolaat nods.

The next course is served, and once again my plate has something a little different from the other guests—a soft grain and vegetable dish topped with a cream sauce. It's rather delicious, actually, and I make short work of it. And then they bring a third course.

"So, your Amrevet Days are going well?" Sheolaat asks me with a lighter expression.

How do I even begin to express? I pause before answering, feeling a slight flush in my cheeks. My treacherous imagination immediately conjures up intense moments of intimacy with Aeson . . . our bodies moving against each other, skin rubbing skin, sweat mingling . . . his lean, hard muscles. . . .

I force myself to focus on the present moment. "Things

are . . . excellent. In every sense," I reply. And I try to hold back a naughty smile which I think Sheolaat sees despite my efforts.

Her own lips curve in unspoken understanding. Did I mention how much I like this woman and the entirety of her quiet, perceptive, and somehow amused vibe? Princess Sheolaat is someone I'd like to hang out with at some point. And I really mean it.

Meanwhile, the rest of the table conversation around us is mostly small talk, as the Pharikon talks about local matters, the SPC, the aftermath of the alien war, Earth and its demands on New Deshret, and Rumeiar occasionally whispers things into Aeson's ear. I listen more than speak, which is not my usual gregarious manner, but—it's just that, suddenly, I find myself in a food coma.

Aeson glances at me often, and I can tell he notices how sleepy I've become—dratted hormones.

Oh, crap. . . . And now I also need to pee.

The matron at my side—who has still not introduced herself, pats my arm gently and says, "You are tired . . . yes?"

"A little," I reply, trying to smile, while my eyelids are fluttering beyond my control.

At once the matron uses a very commanding voice to interrupt the Pharikon. "Enough, Arevi—the young woman is exhausted and needs to rest! Let's conclude this meal and let the Imperator and his Wife continue their proper Amrevet Days activities! Matters of state and gossip can wait."

"Harumph!" Pharikon Heru grunts and his narrowed eyes widen momentarily at the interruption. "Very well, yes. . . . The Imperial Wife does appear in need of rest. And you, my boy—Aeson. Let's pick this up another night."

"Thank you for a wonderful *niktos* meal and your gracious company," Aeson says. "Gwen has had a long day, and so have I. Would you like to speak briefly now, before we retire?"

In reply, the Pharikon motions for his servants who approach solicitously to help him rise. "The rest of you, sit, eat, eat!" the old man says loudly to the table in general. "Don't let this stop you from gorging nicely. No food is to go to waste, you hear? *Eat!* I want no leftovers! This Royal House is not as rich as some others, so we must make do and conserve the divine blessings upon us and the good resources. . . ."

The guests heed his skillfully voice-modulated ramblings and continue to eat politely.

I almost giggle, considering that the Pharikon and all of New Deshret is in fact filthy rich. In this tirade, at last, the sly old man I am familiar with, shines through!

Aeson and I stand up, incline our heads decorously to the rest of the guests and, seeing the Pharikon shuffling ahead, follow him to the door, pausing at one of the recessed alcoves near the colonnade.

Here, out of earshot of everyone else, the Pharikon tells his servants to stand away, and then addresses Aeson and me. His expression has become alert and his narrow eyes are sharp and familiar in their forceful energy.

"Listen, young Kassiopei, and you, Gwen," he says. "I am abdicating my throne. Very, very soon. You hear it from me now, before anyone else here. . . . No one knows. . . . Even Sheolaat hasn't heard me say it formally to her, though she suspects the time is nearing."

"Oh?" Aeson says in a careful voice with notes of concern. "Are you—are you feeling well?"

"Yes, yes." Areviktet Heru motions with his hand in slight annoyance. "Sufficiently enough for now, but the dire events of the last year have taken their toll. New, young leadership is needed. Especially with all the demands laid upon all of us in charge of nations, the expansion, the rebuilding. Even with your Earth—" and he glances at me—"now a part of this political equation. In short—change is coming, and more. New Deshret, and your *Atlantida*, and the rest, we have so much work ahead of us, alliances to forge and reinforce—"

"When?" Aeson interrupts gently. "When do you plan to announce?"

"Most likely within this year." The Pharikon exhales, then coughs and speaks plaintively. "I am tired, my boy . . . I've had more than enough of this ruling nonsense. Decades and decades. . . ."

And then he looks at me. "When your child is born, there will very likely be a new Pharikon in New Deshret. And I hope to strengthen the bond between our nations in some more concrete manner. Let your child, your first-born Heir—girl or boy—marry one of ours. I have several three-year-old younglings running around the Palace, offspring of some distant cousins, of just the right age for your little Heir—"

I almost choke.

"It's a profound honor," Aeson says calmly. "And your offer makes good sense and follows common tradition. But, let's not rush, let the child be born first and make a few choices, before *anyone* decides its fate."

There is a long pause.

And then Pharikon Heru starts to laugh. "Fear not, that infernal tradition—ah, no! I don't mean to impose it on the young. I wanted to poke you a little, both of you, on your Amrevet Days! Now, go, get out of here, enjoy yourselves!"

And then, switching mercurially back to serious, he adds. "The abdication part is not a joke. Keep it to yourselves."

I bite my lip. "We will," I mutter. "Of course."

"Go! Your Guest Quarters has a nice and sturdy bed, feel free to try to break it tonight!"

Dear lord, did he just wink at us?

Aeson and I exchange startled glances—and then, as per our host's command, we get the hell out of there.

. . .

BACK IN OUR GUEST QUARTERS, alone at last, I take a big breath of relief. As I begin to remove my formal clothing, and Aeson does the same, getting ready for bed, I muse out loud: "He seems okay overall, Aeson. But there was that brief lapse when he brought up your Father. . . ."

"I know." Aeson pauses to glance at me as he unbuttons his expensive shirt, while his formal gold collar has been deposited at a side table nearby. "I am saddened to see the subtle changes starting in him. Areviktet is a good man."

"He is." I nod, then move in closer to Aeson and put my hands over his as he works the clasps.

"Let's thank our Host for these nice accommodations," my Imperial Husband says, turning his full attention to me. He looks into my eyes and his own reveal the familiar darkened pupils. "And let us not think of sad things now, because after all, these are our Amrevet Days. And sorrow must be discarded for the duration."

"Agreed," I whisper, pulling the rest of his shirt off to bare his gorgeous muscular shoulders. I slide my hands around his neck and wrap myself around him. My baby bump presses gently at his abdomen while, just below, I feel an immediate bulge growing in his pants.

"You promised to screw me . . ." I say in his ear, hiding my face in his golden hair.

"Not so sleepy now, are you, *im vuchusei?*"

I make some kind of unintelligible noise between a giggle and a snort.

Aeson's powerful arms come around me and he squeezes me, a little too hard, but I'm already turning to melted honey in his embrace.

His hands slide lower, cupping my rear, and his voice is deep and serpentine, and so very *penetrating*, as he speaks, hot breath tickling my neck. "As promised . . . I'm about to *varqood* your brains out."

CHAPTER 7

"Oh, is *that* what you're going to do to me, mister?" I ask coyly, starting to press my lips against his skin, near the back of his ear . . . over and over . . . while I move my hands up and down the back of his neck and shoulders, stroking him with a combination of gentle pressure and sensuality.

But Aeson pulls me back away from himself so that he can face me and *look* at me—or rather, so that I can see his expression —and there is a very wicked smile on his lips.

And just like that, his smile is gone.

I'm still wearing the silky sheath portion of my dress, the innermost layer that's wrapped like gossamer against my body. It has built-in bra support, but otherwise is sleeveless, sheer, and nearly translucent enough to reveal my body to my husband as he watches me with unblinking gravity.

Goosebumps. . . .

We're both standing not far from the oversized luxury bed, and I glance behind us at its soft coverlets and pillows, and of course he understands my look without the need for words.

This is the point at which I would normally expect him to

pick me up and carry me to the bed, then set me down with utmost care, as if I were some kind of pregnant hothouse flower.

But Aeson manages to surprise me yet again.

"Gwen," he says in a soft, mesmerizing, power voice. *"Remove the rest of your clothes. Then . . . get on the bed."*

I know it's not the compelling voice, but it very well could be. Lately I've noticed that Aeson seems to naturally express the raw power of the compelling voice when he is deeply aroused.

"Okay . . ." I reply softly. Without another word, I take the hem of my translucent sheath and then pull it up and over my head, liberating my breasts. Next, I pull down my panties, step out of them and pick them up, not sure why. Completely naked, with my boobs swaying, I straighten and continue to hold both garments in my hands as I back away from him—never looking away from his face, feeling his serpentine, masculine scrutiny pressing upon me like a tangible wall of electricity. . . .

Three steps and I bump against the bed with the back of my thighs, feel the softness of the coverlet behind me. I let go of the clothes, letting them fall onto the bed nearby, then sit down and slowly scoot over with my naked rear end until I am in the middle of the bed.

"Now, you," I say, staring at him. My husband is beautiful like a god, naked to the waist, and currently has a very big tent in the crotch of his pants.

Aeson stands motionless, watching my movements. And now, prompted by me, he undoes his formal pants and kicks off his shoes.

And then he is naked also, his big dick pointing at me.

"Come, Aeson," I say, patting the coverlet next to me.

"I will soon," he replies with double entendre, slowly approaching me. I look at his shaft, and the tip is already beading and glistening with the impending pre-cum.

He pauses at the edge of the bed, standing there, watching me in silence. Then he slowly leans forward and places both hands on the coverlet, on either side of me. His cock rests against the covers, twitching.

I stare at the Imperial Serpent, feeling a pulse start up inside me.

"So beautiful. . . . What am I going to do with you?" he asks in a low, rich voice that breaks hoarsely.

And then he puts his hands on me, spreading apart my thighs, and I let him, sinking backward on the bed.

The Imperator advances, sliding closer and climbs on the bed. He then grips my hips on both sides and pulls me to him, while I moan with anticipation, leaving my legs wide open, my rounded belly facing up.

Aeson puts his hands on my inner thighs, his strong fingers going soft and gentle over my skin. He stokes me with the palms of his hands, his touch deepening, and then leans directly down with his head and puts his hot mouth on me . . . right *there*.

And he begins to eat me.

His glorious golden hair falls loosely over me, covering me, while his lips suck and gently pull at my clit. His tongue laps and sweeps around it, and my body arches and pulses with each rhythmic pull.

I clutch his hair, long silk strands, beautiful liquid gold... and I dig my fingers into his scalp convulsively, because I am being turned inside out and wrung with pain-pleasure. An overwhelming irrational need of pulling him inside me makes me press his head closer, even as he works me, and I moan with every breath, drowning in electric waves, until I squeeze my eyes shut and climax, riding into him, hard.

Even before I'm done convulsing, he lifts his face, his lips glistening, and pushes me deeper onto the bed, his strong hands and arms sliding against my hips and waist, so that I am shifted backwards against the mountain of pillows.

"Was it good, *im vuchusei?*"

"Yes," I whisper, regaining my breath. "So good. But I still have my brains." My voice flirts wickedly, and I smile at him, daring him to do more.

Aeson looks at me with a steady gaze, and his pupils are dilated, turning his dark blue eyes to midnight. And then he begins to crawl toward me, and covers me with his strength and heat. His hard abdomen presses lightly against my belly, so that I feel the warmth of his skin, but he keeps his torso controlled and elevated enough not to rest his full weight on me.

Feeling relaxed after my release, all my limbs like molten honey, I put my arms around his shoulders and muscular upper arms in an instinctive embrace. But just in that moment my breath is suspended, and I have to gasp, because suddenly he thrusts hard between my parted thighs, impaling me.... The instant surge of pleasure is unbelievable, followed by the familiar fullness as his big cock opens me up on the inside and starts to glide, in and out, invoking the mechanism of primeval creation.

I forget how much of a surge of raw emotional longing can come over me in those moments whenever we are mated together. Every single time, without fail, it is a moment of perfect being, of buzzing life force, the engine of perpetual motion equal only to the one time when Aeson and I were joined mind-to-mind by the trans-dimensional miracle of the *pegasei*, and discovered the glory of each other. We lived a lifetime in a single breath, and this physical joining, here and now, recalls the intimacy of our souls blending, and evokes the almost painful echo of that *oneness*....

The wistful, bittersweet memory of that joining rises up for one ephemeral moment, casting an iridescent wonder over the present, and then recedes into the shadows of the mind while the carnal sensuality takes over, the physical roaring fire of the flesh....

And oh, how it burns! We burn together, moving, and

grinding, and I grip his body, as close as possible to mine, while he buries himself in me, over and over, plunging and sowing and destroying me with the act of love.

At some point, Aeson shudders and stops moving. I hear his deep groan, and his voice breaking out of control, as he ejaculates.

Moments later he resumes moving, fierce and dark with focus, and his bottomless gaze bores into me until I come again, my vaginal walls clenching around him.

My mind breaks and reforms.

My husband leans his golden head near my ear and whispers in a remarkably controlled voice near my cheek, even as his lower body continues pumping in and out of me, "And now, *im vuchusei*, how are your brains doing?"

In reply I mutter something unintelligible, because I am a mess of satiation and ringing senses, and my mouth has trouble forming words.

Aeson smiles joyfully, oh-so-wickedly, and then he stifles my attempt at communication with his own mouth hard against my lips, until I am absolutely senseless indeed.

SOMETIME LATER, as we lie together in a mess of pillows and coverlets and sticky entwined limbs, I look up at the gorgeous ceiling of the guest chamber and point out one architectural detail or another and ask nonsensical questions.

"Is that a swirly star or a flower, Aeson?" I mumble.

"Neither," he replies, playfully tapping my bottom lip, or lightly caressing my belly. "It's a stylized cloud. Original Deshi style."

"Oh, is that what it is?" I say, then press my cheek even closer, rubbing myself against his chest. "What about these draping valances or curtain thingies over those niches? Such pretty, shimmering, green and rose fabric, like mother of pearl."

"Like mother of what?" he asks, turning my chin up with his large strong fingers to look at me. My Imperial Husband occasionally admits to not knowing certain English words, which I find almost shocking, considering how flawless his English is otherwise. But then, it occurs to me in the next instant, he could be simply teasing me.

"It has those different iridescent colors," I say. "A little like the *pegasei*."

A soft smile comes to his lips. "Ah, yes," he says. And then he adds, "It's quite possible the fabric and the decor were inspired by *pegasei* in the ancient days."

"Oh! Is that how old these curtains are?" I exclaim, lifting my head to look up at him.

He chuckles. "No, these are modern. But the style is traditional. Most likely, as per instructions of the Pharikon's Queen Consort."

An interesting notion occurs to me. As far as I know, the current Pharikon, Areviktet Heru, has no spouse or children. So, I ask Aeson.

Aeson thinks briefly before answering. "It's true, Areviktet has no Queen. It's somewhat complicated."

"How so?"

Aeson brings one hand around, squeezing me, and rubs the back of my neck. "Heru was married to a woman of high nobility a long time ago, a formal arranged marriage, as dictated by Protocol. He was forced to it by duty and the confines of his rank. It is rumored it was deeply against his will, but he of course never admitted it in public, nor would the Heru Family permit such a lapse. The marriage was barren, with no offspring, and the Queen Consort died soon, quite young."

"Oh, no," I say.

"It was so long ago, several generations before ours. I was told that Areviktet's royal parents tried to have him remarried, but this time he denied them outright, and remained unwed for the rest of his time."

"How sad, I am so sorry to hear," I say. "I wonder why?"

"So many court rumors in that regard." Aeson draws circles with his thumb around one of my breasts, closing in around the tip. "Some thought him to be overly discriminating, or stubborn, or contrary, or *amrechiro*, preferring other men. Other rumors eventually came to light, but only decades later. Areviktet had loved only one woman all his life, and she was deemed unsuitable to be Queen Consort. Apparently, after Queen Kiadis, his wife, died, he informed his Family that he has done his duty to his Dynasty once and that was enough. Since he could not marry his love, he would not marry anyone else at all."

I listen intently, almost stopping breathing. "This is so sad, it's even worse."

But Aeson tweaks my nipple then presses his lips against my forehead. "It is not so sad, don't worry," he tells me. "Areviktet has kept his love close to him for all these years. She has borne him three children if not more, though unfortunately none of them can inherit the Deshi Throne."

"Oh!" I say with a surge of relief. "Where is she? Does she live in the Palace with him?"

"You've met her." Aeson chuckles again. "The woman seated next to you at our *niktos* meal tonight."

"That older matron!" I exclaim. "Oh, wow, I never even asked her name, and was unsure if she was maybe his relative, a sister or cousin."

"She is Areviktet's wife in all but law. For all practical purposes, Dame Uharida Mehgla runs his household and is a wonderful woman."

"Why in the world would she be unsuitable?"

"She's a former *amretene*—a courtesan, but of the most ordinary, lowest class."

I muse for a moment in silence. "This is the kind of nonsense that ruins human happiness," I say.

"Agreed. But it's the result of their ancient laws."

I shake my head. "Why is it always that human laws lag behind human cultural progress and civilization? Laws are supposed to be there to serve us, not the other way around."

Before Aeson can reply, his wrist unit makes a ringing tone. He checks it with a glance, then looks at me with a slow mischievous smile. "Good news, *im amrevu*. They've captured and properly fed our new cat. We will see it when we get back to our *depet*."

CHAPTER 8: AESON

G wen doesn't know I'm writing this.

I decided, recently, to write a chronicle of some of my personal experiences, not unlike her own intimate record of *self* —what the Gebi call a "diary." It is, I believe, a natural extension of that original task that I assigned her on board ICS-2 (so long ago now, it seems) of keeping a historical record, from a Gebi perspective, of the Earth Mission's return journey to Atlantis.

Over the past few weeks, she has hinted that she plans to continue writing down her experiences—not for public perusal, but of a more personal nature. She even mentioned a rather vivid and historically meaningful title for her record: *The Book of Everything*.

At first, I suspected that she had already started it, because I've seen her scribbling in a very old-fashioned Earth-style journal when she thought no one was watching. But now I'm not entirely certain that is what she's writing.

Yes, I admit it, I stare at her often, observe her—sometimes foolishly, in secret—like a besotted lover, not wanting to intrude upon her private time but somehow unable to keep away, even though we're formally joined as Husband and Wife and there's absolutely no need for it. And what I see is enchanting. . . . Judging by the spontaneous giggles she produces, the delightful way she puts the end of her writing instrument in her mouth and pauses periodically, almost in an erotic daze, then quickly stops and hides the journal when I make my presence known— this particular thing is of an even more *intimate* nature than I suspected.

I'm extremely amused.

Gwen, ah, Gwen. . . . *Im vuchusei amrevu.*

There are no words intense enough to express what I feel for her—and our child growing inside her.

She breaks me open with a single clear-eyed glance and devastates me with her smile. Even now, after all our months together, I look at her and I *melt*. I want to be with her, to kiss her, devour her. . . . It's not my Kassiopei physical urge driving me, so much as the soul connection between us, that strange, unbreakable bond that makes us one greater spirit on some impossible, extra-dimensional level. The *pegasei* communion we've shared for a brief, glorious moment, merely brought it into sharper focus. That one experience of *no walls between our minds* fused us together for endless lifetimes. . . . But we were already bound, long before.

Enough, I need to stop.

Rather, I need to channel my fierce love into a constructive, tangible thing. Hence, this narrative.

I BEGIN my chronicle at the start of our Amrevet Days, on the first night, when we're guests of the Pharikon of New Deshret. After a remarkable day of intimacy and blessed peace and quiet at the ruins and desert spring aqueducts of Anun-Xaat in Heruvar (a location I chose intentionally so that we could splash naked in those glorious freshwater pools), we head to Xois to attend the evening reception at Court. It is good as always to see the astute old man Areviktet Heru, without undue formality and international politics marring our interactions, and to catch up with my heart brother Rumeiar.

We enjoy excellent company and a genuinely pleasant *niktos* meal at the Deshi Royal Palace, culminating in some extremely pleasurable bedroom activity in our Guest Quarters. And in the morning, both Gwen and I wake up well rested, quite early, and return to our *nubu depet*.

It's time to continue our global journey.

When we enter our own Quarters on the *depet*, Gwen lets out a little scream of joy. There's a cat curled up in an *eos*-pie-roll shape right in the middle of the living room sofa. That same silver-white creature from the Anun-Xaat aqueducts, lean and beautifully wild. Of course, the moment that Gwen's delightful Logos voice erupts, the cat bolts from its spot and disappears underneath the sofa.

"Oh, no!" *im amrevu* says, with a soft laugh, putting a hand over her mouth. "Oh shoot, I scared it!" she adds in a loud whisper, then attempts to bend down, in order to look for it under the furniture. "Kitty! Here, kitty!"

"Don't worry about it," I say, watching my Wife stop halfway and freeze, as if recalling that she now has a small belly that might make it somewhat uncomfortable to crouch this way. She then holds on to her abdomen with one hand, considering how to proceed.

"Let's be very quiet!" Gwen finally decides which way to move and sits down on the sofa, with her feet together, almost in a military stance of readiness (to pounce?) and puts a finger over her mouth to indicate silence.

"It will come out eventually," I say, approaching, and stand with my arms folded as I look down at her with amusement. "There's really nowhere for it to go. In fact, the best thing to do now is ignore it and let it get used to our rooms and our smells."

Gwen sighs and bites her lower lip. "I realize that. I just feel bad for crying out and waking it when it looked so cozy. At least we know they fed it—right?"

"Right. The steward reported to me that they fed it extremely well—it ate everything. And only then did they place the creature in our Quarters, along with water and a box for its elimination needs."

"Where is the litter box?" Gwen looks up at me. "Is it in our bathroom? Will the cat know how to use it?"

"Yes. It's been properly sprayed with pheromones, so all is handled."

"Okay. . . ."

I smile at her and her fidgeting worry. Gwen smiles back at me, but then puts her finger over her lips again and widens her eyes. "Shhh! Come, sit here with me, and let's see if it comes out!"

I sit down next to her and place my right arm around the sofa back, from where I can easily reach Gwen's neck and play with her soft brown hair. Then I glance down at the wrist unit on my left hand to check the messages, in case any formal Imperial business communications arrived. Fortunately, there's nothing of major import.

While I'm briefly occupied thus, Gwen periodically makes soothing sounds and whispers, "Hi, kitty . . . don't be scared . . . good kitty cat. . . ." From the corner of my eye, I note she continues to keep her feet very still, as if any movement would disturb the furry occupant beneath our seats.

"So, where are we heading next?" *im amrevu* finally asks, touching my upper arm softly. The contact with her hand sends an immediate prickling current of sensual *awareness* along my arm.

I look up from my messages, and then glance at the oversized observation windows that show a motionless blinding daylight view of the Royal Palace airfield outside our *depet*. We're still hover-parked in Xois, New Deshret, since I haven't issued the command to the captain in regard to our next destination.

"Well," I say, "Since we're still in New Deshret, there's Dubutaat Mountain not too far from here, where the Golden Ra Disk is installed. Want to see it? It's an amazing sight, up-close."

"Hm-m-m. . . ." Gwen furrows her forehead.

"We don't have to, of course," I add.

"Well, no, I *want* to see it, at some point. Maybe just not now. It makes me think of the whole Grail Monument business, with the awful quantum ringing alarm across the universe that we just couldn't disable no matter how we tried."

"I understand completely," I say, recalling the Great Quantum Shield, and our Plural Voice Chorus of three Logos voices intertwined into a thing of beauty and power. . . . With a pang of painful, dark emotion, I think of my Father, singing with us. "We'll skip it for now."

"Let's get out of New Deshret," Gwen says. "Let's return closer to home, to Imperial *Atlantida*. How about we go way north, near the Pole of Ra? For some ridiculous reason, I really want to visit the Chicken Sea!"

"The—what?" I raise one brow. And then I recall. "Ah yes, the Hebu Sea."

Gwen laughs, and her lovely eyes brighten, making me secretly catch my breath with a warm surge of delight as I look at her. "The silly name that we Earthies gave it, I know. But you've got to admit, looking from above, it does have the outline of a chicken!"

I shake my head and keep my lips from quivering at the corners as I raise one brow. "It wouldn't be the first thing that comes to mind when I look at it, but—yes, apparently you Gebi seem to enjoy the joke. And all of you also apparently really like chicken. Poor birds. . . ."

Gwen punches me on my arm with a mocking burst of outrage. She then drops the silly act and leans closer to rest her head against my chest before straightening to stare earnestly into my eyes with unmistakable adoration.

Ah, that look, I know it so well. . . . Her eyes. . . . Such perfectly clear blue eyes.

With a surge of emotion followed by instant heat, I lower my head and press my lips against hers instinctively. . . . She immediately opens her mouth. My kiss deepens. I feel her fingers slide through my hair and into the back of my scalp as she pulls me in closer.

For several heartbeats we are both lost. . . .

Mingled breathing. . . . Light, tiny moans starting.

It's the eventuality of all things related to our physical contact, that I feel myself hardening below.

Reluctantly I break apart from her, wipe my mouth with the back of my hand and smile into her eyes. "All right, Chicken Sea it is. That's in Eos-Heket. I'm sure the Oratorat will be happy to see us."

But Gwen slides her hand down and she puts it on my crotch, directly over my pulsing *varqooi*. "I think someone else is happy to see us," she says to me with dilated, heavy-lidded eyes and a teasing smile. "I don't want to startle the cat under us with . . . um . . . shifting furniture, so—onto the bed, *now*, Big Boy!"

JUST A FEW RUSHED, semi-stumbling steps, and we're in our bedroom, on top of our large, *sturdy* bed.

Gwen crawls on the covers and grabs a few of the pillows to fluff, then rests backward against them. She starts unbuttoning the top of her dress. It's one of her loose, pull-on ones, but the bodice has a few fasteners. Instead of assisting her, I take advantage of glimpses of her creamy skin and sink my mouth against those spots, tasting her flavor, her unique scent, sucking deeply, while my *varqooi* grows even harder, and I press into her from below, my hands fumbling to open her thighs.

There's no time to lift her dress over her head. She hitches her skirts up, over her waist, baring her legs and—there are her silk panties. Before I can see her sweet crotch and spread her *amreh*, the infernal female undergarments must be eliminated.

I pause briefly, sit back on my knees, and start undoing the front of my own pants, giving her a few urgent moments to roll down the panties past her knees, and get them off one leg at least, before we resume the erotic fumble.

Gwen is breathing fast already. At last, she's completely naked below, and sits cross-legged, opening her *amreh* to me.

The front of my pants pops open, and my *varqooi* pushes out, fully engorged and twitching, pointing almost completely up. . . . No time to remove my shirt or the rest of my clothes; right now, I'm so hard I could burst.

That's when I see my Wife undo the front clasp of her bra, releasing her large, beautiful pair of *sohuru*. At once they fall out past the unbuttoned dress bodice and slide down to repose against her rounded belly, with nipples immediately protruding, revealing her degree of arousal.

I stop and stare, mesmerized. Then I grasp her *sohuru* in my hands, soft and plump and wonderfully heavy. I run my thumbs against the hard tips, then put my head down and take them in my mouth, one at a time. Wide-mouthed, I suck in her nipples, take them in all the way past the areolae. I lightly pull with my teeth then suck again, rhythmically . . . and in moments Gwen begins to moan in a loud, husky voice, throwing her head back against the pile of pillows.

"Ah . . ." I groan deeply between each breath, massaging the *sohuru* flesh on the sides, squeezing them together.

"Aeson!" she exclaims breathlessly, stopping me for a moment. She then smiles at me, panting suggestively, and pushes her *sohuru* together with her own hands, offering them up to me. "Want to come between my tits?" she whispers, opening her mouth and licking her lips. "I know you want to. . . ."

She then leans down and thoroughly lubricates the tops of her *sohuru* with her tongue, until they glisten. . . .

I groan again.

"Go ahead, put your Big Boy right here, between my tits, and . . . I'll catch you with my mouth—"

In answer, I'm right *there*. . . .

I stick my *varqooi* in the crevice between her warm, rotund flesh, and I start pumping vigorously, my fingers squeezing her prominent *sohuru* from both sides, riding against their well-padded width and into her mouth.

Each time the bulb of my *varqooi* nears her mouth, she moves her tongue quickly to lap at the tip that's already leaking. . . . She licks up the drops of pre-cum, once, twice . . . again and again, giving me exquisite shots of pleasure with each quick, unexpected stroke.

The orgasm hits. I tighten, groan uncontrollably, then go off into her face, with such power that my cum spills white all around her mouth, chin, cheeks, spraying her *sohuru*, while she shuts her eyes, giggles, and moans, simultaneously parting her lips wide, lapping with her tongue.

"Holy jizz, Aeson! You really unloaded this one!" she exclaims, still blinking, wiping her face and starting to laugh.

"Sorry . . . sorry!" I grasp out, still catching my breath.

"I know you like my boobs, but this is ridiculous," she continues, using a nearby towel to clean her face—and chest that jiggles invitingly even now, from the smallest of her movements.

I shake my head helplessly, grinning at her, ogling her bouncing pair. "All right, this time let me come inside you."

"If there's anything *left* in you, after that!" she responds smartly. "Sure, please do come inside me, my Imperial Husband! Because I'd like to come too!"

. . .

READY AGAIN, only five heartbeats later, I mount her, as always, carefully restraining the range of my motion over her pregnant belly.

As I begin to pump inside her tight, profoundly lubricated *amreh*, it occurs to me, when I moved between her *sohuru* just now, I didn't hold back. In that placement, I was never worried about pushing too hard against the baby, possibly for the first time in months. That might explain some of my extreme *excretions*, shall we say.

Of course, there's the simple fact that her *sohuru* are spectacular.

A dozen strokes later, I give my sweet Gwen a proper orgasm. Her vaginal walls contract rhythmically around the length of me, so there's no hiding it—even though she purses her lips at me in a cute pretense of annoyance and attempts to stifle her usual high-pitched moan and remain entirely silent . . . this time.

No such luck, *im vuchusei*.

She squeezes her eyes shut and, as the reflex motion begins, her hips buck intensely around me, while her *amreh* pulses out of control with the pleasure waves.

In that moment, *im amrevu* cries out, deliciously, as always.

The sonorous sound of her Logos voice breaks me.

And it makes me come hard, yet again.

SOMETIME LATER, we lounge on top of the bed covers, semi-naked, full of sweet lassitude, covered with the usual sticky mess, mostly of my own making. *Bashtooh*, all that infernal Kassiopei seed. . . . This bed will need to be cleaned before evening. So much sex and it's still mid-morning.

Also, we probably gave our timid new cat—hiding

somewhere in the next room—another grand show. But then, considering how it first found us, it should be used to it.

"Aeson, we're still parked in New Deshret," Gwen says, poking me in the ribs then tickling my armpit.

I cough and shrink from the tickle, then respond by squeezing her plump rear end. "Yes. Let me call the captain and tell him to set course to Eos-Heket."

"Your wrist thingie is blinking."

"Okay." I glance down at my left wrist, and see a priority message indicator. Ah, *bashtooh*, again. "Could be Imperial business. Let me check this," I say, sobering up momentarily.

I expect some kind of nagging issue from a member of the IEC, but when I open the message text, it's a note from George Lark.

Why is it marked priority?

"What is it?" Gwen asks with concern, seeing the serious change in my expression.

"Hold on," I say. "It's from your brother George."

"What? Did something happen?" Gwen grasps my wrist in alarm.

But as I visually scan the message, I let out a breath of relief. And then a new excitement swells inside me that I can share something like this with Gwen.

"Something *good*." I say, smiling slyly at her. "George received a communication from Earth. It's something really, really good. Are you ready?"

"What? What?" she exclaims, pummeling me. "Tell me already, you jerk!"

"George says that your friend from school, Ann Finnbar is alive and well. And she wants to get in touch with you!"

Gwen gasps, puts both hands over her mouth. And then she screams.

The sound of her *joy*—this particular joy—is even better than the sound of her orgasm.

CHAPTER 9

I n that moment when Aeson tells me that Ann Finnbar is
alive, I am flooded with wild, overwhelming *joy*. Together
with it, comes an unexpected sense of relief from a deeply-
buried and suppressed sense of foreboding that's been
malingering inside me all this time—a dark fear relegated to the
background, something I haven't been consciously aware of, for
all these endless months. . . .

In the back of my mind, I've irrationally held on to the
delusional hope that *everyone* I knew who had been left behind,
including my old school friend, was somehow *okay*. That hope
remained bound, in a weak, loose thread of emotional affinity,
with everything else that represented my younger self—Earth,
Vermont, my high school, my classmates, our old home—
despite the apocalyptic horrors of what had been happening
there. . . .

No, stop. . . .

So many people had perished on Earth since we left. I know
that. That's the hard reality. . . . And if I didn't dwell on the past
too closely, I could continue to pretend that nothing changed.

Especially since we managed to prevent the asteroid impact and the extinction.

But now, hearing from Ann, slams all my magically preserved past back into existence—that long-suspended hope mixed with bitter, secret suspicion that no one could've made it through the fiery hell that was Earth after the Atlantean Fleet left.

But *this* is no longer a delusion, this is real.

Ann is alive! And she reached out to me from Earth via George!

My brain processes in seconds all this amazing news, and so of course I shriek and cover my mouth, while Aeson watches my reaction in delight.

"Aeson, *what?*" I scream. "Oh my God! *Ann!* Ann Finnbar? She is okay! She survived! What did George say?"

Aeson chuckles, stroking my shoulder casually, because we're still naked and sprawled in our bed. "Not much," he replies. "George didn't want to bother us during our Amrevet Days, but this was just too good to postpone. He says that Ann and her family are all safe at their home in Vermont and she simply wanted to speak to you at some point, via interstellar comms."

"Oh wow, yes!" I say, grinning with excitement. "I'll call George! I'll tell him—"

"Not right *now*, I hope," my Imperial Husband says with amusement, pointing to my boobs. "Not unless you want to show your brother some of that lovely naked—"

"*No!* Eeow!" I swat Aeson's upper arm and make a mocking face of horror. But I continue to grin. "Okay, I'll call him this afternoon."

"No rush. Ann is not going anywhere. And she must know, by now, some of your circumstances, so she would understand your delay in replying."

Aeson runs one hand lightly over my baby belly, and gently

massages the skin. He leans in and kisses it gently—our *baby* inside. Then he calls the captain of our *nubu depet* and tells him to set course for our next romantic destination, this one in Eos-Heket.

We're going far north and back to our home hemisphere on the opposite side of the planet, to see that infamous body of water that we Earthies decided to call "the Chicken Sea."

ACCORDING TO AESON, the Hebu Sea stays frozen for most of the year. Except for its funny shape, I know very little about it from my original Atlantean geography classes. Now, I get to find out a whole lot more.

In minutes—pardon me, daydreams—we rise from the Royal Deshi Palace airfield, and soar upward with dizzying speed. Xois, the capital city, and all of New Deshret falls away, as we breach the upper atmosphere. And then we fly north toward the Pole of Ra, but with a slight westward declination.

I love watching the strange, sudden color and light changes outside our grand view port windows. The brightness of Helfire inside the thick atmosphere is replaced by deep indigo and cosmic black as we skim the edges of space, sending blue shadows racing across our cabin interior. And then we plummet back down into the blinding daylight.

All of this happens while we're still lounging comfortably in the soft luxury of our bed. In addition, the ride in our *nubu depet* is extraordinarily smooth and the environmental variation outside is hardly noticeable.

"The sky of Atlantis is so gorgeous, Aeson," I say, my gaze following the rapid transition of the color spectrum outside the observation windows.

Im amrevu stretches his arms behind him in utmost relaxation. He is naked and muscular, powerful like a lion with his golden mane of hair, and he rests back against the pillows next to me. He glances at the blazing sky, then at me, with a lazy, heavy-lidded look of sensuality.

And he merely smiles.

Just then, a furry silver cat muzzle appears at the doorway, peering carefully inside our bed chamber. The cat! Finally, the kitty has decided to reveal itself and investigate!

"Sh-h-h . . ." I whisper to Aeson, growing absolutely still, and then motioning with my head at the open door into our living room. "Look who's here! *Don't move!*"

"I know." Aeson widens his eyes meaningfully at me. "It's been watching us for a while now. Popping in to look, then hiding again."

"Oh, so cute!" I whisper, holding back a giggle of delight. "Look at that little face! All right, not that little, but still, cute big muzzle!"

At the sound of my excited whisper, the cat's ears perk up, and it stares directly at me. Then, after another sufficient pause, it begins to slowly advance into our bedroom, keeping to the wall perimeter.

"Wow, look how big he is—or she! I think it's looking for more food."

"Or for the elimination box," Aeson whispers, humoring me. "It seems to be moving toward the bathroom."

A few slow and stealthy movements later, the kitty indeed disappears into the open doorway leading into the bathroom suite, holding its belly and tail low to the ground.

"What name will you give it?" Aeson glances at me.

I think for a moment. "We don't know if it's a girl or boy yet. But, just looking at so much silvery gray fur, and such pretty, golden eyes, makes me think of *orichalcum*. In other words, grey and gold together! So, what if we call it Ohri?"

"Hm-m-m, Ohri," Aeson repeats. "A solid name. I like it."

"Great!" I smile and try out the name, not expecting anything. "Ohri! Ohri! Come here, Ohri!"

Aeson shakes his head in amusement. "Give it time."

"Oh, I plan to, mister. This kitty will know exactly what Ohri means. Food and *love*."

"I expect, also much flatulence," my Imperial Husband mumbles, holding back laughter.

WHILE OUR SHIP descends toward Eos-Heket, Aeson and I decide to clean up and shower. We tiptoe into the bathroom, trying to not surprise the cat. However, the smart feline has either managed to slip out past us and is no longer there, or it's hiding again in some incomprehensible, clever manner. The litterbox looks untouched, and so do the food and water dishes.

Typical wary cat behavior.

So, we get on with our bathroom business. Aeson runs the water in the shower while I brush my teeth, then join him in the luxuriously large enclosure. We start to frolic for a bit, until we orgasm under the cascading water, then scrub each other's backs.

When we're done, we step outside and grab enormous fluffy towels from a stack nearby, and . . . there's Ohri the cat, curled up underneath the third towel.

"There you are!" I say, leaning forward with my belly and dripping water. "Ohri!"

Ohri gives a short hiss, then streaks away, escaping from the bathroom and back into our bedroom.

"Aww, all right. This is going to take a while," I say.

"Feral creature. Perfectly normal." Aeson wrings out his long mane of hair and tosses it carelessly behind him, then picks up his towel. Meanwhile I cannot help but stare at his perfectly defined abdomen, wide shoulders, toned upper arms, and all that glistening bronzed skin. . . . His muscles flex gorgeously with every one of his motions as he dries himself.

Talk about a feral creature. . . .

I feel a surge of heat again as I pause to observe the beautiful male specimen before me. Lord help me, didn't we just do it in the shower, moments ago? I am insatiable for him! Must be my heightened hormones.

I still can't believe he's mine.

My husband. . . .

Aeson notices the nature of my look and wiggles one raven-dark brow at me. "Let's have some late *eos* bread first," he says. "Or early *dea* meal, whichever you prefer. You—and the baby—need to recharge before we resume our—ahem—pleasant activities—"

"With Ohri as our sole witness. . . . And sure, food sounds really good right about now." I make a little happy sound and then wrap myself in my towel and head back to our bedroom. Aeson follows.

AN AMAZING SIGHT greets us outside the observation windows of our bedroom cabin. While we showered, our *nubu depet* has landed and hover-parked itself in the middle of what appears to be a boundless ocean. . . . It has waters so dark they appear to be almost black, with tints of turquoise and mauve glittering along the barely stirring surface.

In less than a quarter-hour we've traveled halfway up the planet, and here it is near sunset. The sky—what we can see of it from this vantage of our windows—is teal, with gradations of peach and rose along small patches of distant clouds. They are painted by Hel, sinking toward the horizon but out of view of our windows.

The *nubu depet* is hovering a few feet above the surface, silent and graceful, and it casts a dark shadow upon the waters.

And then, I see the floating peaks of whiteness, rising in places like pale islands from the *niktos* waters.

"Icebergs," Aeson tells me, seeing my silent, awed stare.

"The Hebu Sea is starting to freeze along the northern parts this time of the year, and soon most of it will be covered with an ice crust. However, it never quite freezes completely.

"So, this is the Hebu Sea," I say. "The deep color of the water is amazing . . . like jewels, like Pegasus Blood."

"Yes, exactly. Though, the darkness is deceptive, as you will see in the morning."

"And so very still. . . . Hardly any waves."

"It's a calm day. But it can get quite stormy here, sometimes." Aeson stands next to me, then points out something in the distance. "See that band of silver haze along the distant horizon? That's part of the northern shoreline, frozen over. It extends into a long northern inlet that stretches almost all the way to the Pole of Ra—the thin area of water near the head or beak of your so-called chicken. But right now, we're right in the middle of the sea."

"In the general belly area of the chicken," I mumble with a little smile.

Aeson chuckles. "Indeed! But now we are going to fly in the opposite direction, south-west, toward the southern-most shore, or the chicken foot. There is something there I want to show you."

"What is it?" I ask looking up at Aeson with a soft smile.

"A nice surprise," he responds, then uses his wrist unit to call the captain and give specific directions.

A few moments later, the *depet* lurches gently and takes off, rising only slightly higher over the waters. It then rotates so that we're facing forward and can now see most of the western sunset—and streaks away, putting even more distance between us and the northern shoreline.

We move smoothly but at incredible speed, so that the sparkle of the waters turns into a single blur of reflected light as we traverse it.

And then the shores start to encroach on both sides as we

enter the narrow inlet portion, until we see the most southern point at the horizon where the Hebu Sea ends and the continent begins.

There, at the very tip of the shore (not more than a small bay), rises a bright vertical structure. From the distance it resembles a craggy needle with a strange glowing tip. As we draw near, it turns into an obelisk, and then resolves into a tower, roughly hewn and ancient, formed from the pale rocks of the shore, and at least in part, orichalcum—because it blazes with Hel-fire in the sunset.

The tower is topped by a great glowing orb, or sphere, possibly glass or transparent crystal. It is a dome of some kind, the bulb of a great lantern—perfectly smooth as we get closer, and glowing with an inner light, at the same time as it appears to reflect the setting light of Hel.

"What in the world is that?" I ask.

Aeson turns to give me a curious look, and his eyes are sparkling with energy.

"The Ancient Hebu Lighthouse," he says, releasing a tense breath. "But—you also know it under a different name on Earth —the Pharos Lighthouse of Alexandria."

"*What?*" I exclaim, putting my hands over my mouth, shocked for the second time in the same day. "No! But—that's impossible! The Pharos Lighthouse was only built at the time of Alexander the Great, around the third century B.C.E.! That's closer to our time, not your deep Atlantean antiquity! It's one of the Seven Wonders of the Ancient World—"

Aeson continues to smile, nodding at me. "Yes, during the Earth Mission I recall studying some of your more recent ancient Earth history—rather faulty, revisionist, and incomplete. What you don't know is that the *original* Pharos Lighthouse was twice as tall and infinitely older than what your history tells you. It was erected more than twelve thousand years ago on the continent of Ancient Atlantis, to mark the southern tip of the landmass on the shore of the Atlantic Ocean. And it was made almost entirely of orichalcum."

My jaw drops.

"When our ancestors fled Earth, they apparently took the Lighthouse apart, stripped it of most of the orichalcum stones, and took it with them, as much as they could fit on their ships. They also took the top section of the Lighthouse, that beautiful crystal dome. What was left of the masonry must've been saved by whoever stayed behind, somehow transported to your more recent site, and rebuilt on a lesser scale in Alexandria."

"Holy crap . . ." I whisper. "I need to tell Dad about this! He would go insane with happiness to see another ancient wonder!"

"*Amre-Ter* Charles will be delighted indeed," Aeson says. "But first, *you* will be delighted. We're staying inside the Lighthouse tonight."

CHAPTER 10

W e're fully dressed and consuming a delicious brunch-like combination of foods that are served interchangeably at both *eos* bread and *dea* meals, as we enjoy the striking sunset view outside our windows. Because of the drastic time zone change—or rather, latitude change, since we've traveled not only west but the vertical distance of most of a hemisphere in what feels like a blink—this meal will now also have to be considered a *niktos* meal. We're suddenly near the Pole of Ra, and the hours of daylight are limited. Honestly, this Atlantean equivalent of abbreviated or "reverse jetlag" is even more confusing than what happens during air travel back on Earth. And now, the *nubu depet* levitates gently past a rocky shoreline and sails onto the beach at the foot of the Lighthouse.

Our ship comes to a hover-stop near several small structures that appear modern in comparison to the towering antique ruin before us. I see sparse vegetation along the beach, as the shore gradually rises into cliffs of striated ivory and mauve stone on both sides of this cove. There are also several roads (paved but weathered and old-looking) and artificial illumination coming from the buildings and lights of occasional vehicles hover-parked in the airfield lot nearby.

"Looks like a little town," I say, pleasantly full after consuming my favorite dishes, my fingers wrapped around a warm mug of steaming *lvikao*.

"The settlement is mostly hospitality services for tourists," Aeson replies, dipping a chunk of crusty flatbread into a buttery sauce full of aromatic herbs, then pops it in his mouth. "Although this is the southernmost tip of the Hebu Sea, this part of Eos-Heket is still sparsely populated, compared to the warmer regions further down south. If you look immediately inland, it's mostly undeveloped wilderness, stern, barren landscapes that surround this place. But this bit of shore with the Lighthouse is a popular tourist attraction. People come from all over to climb the hundreds of ancient steps leading up to the top of the tower, just to see the view from the crystal dome."

"Hundreds of steps?"

Aeson nods. "If I recall, there are well over a thousand stone steps leading to the dome. If the tourists are lucky, they get to stay in the quarters overnight. But there's a long waiting list—months in advance—to reserve that main suite of rooms."

"Oh, that's a shame," I say, blissfully shivering in sensory delight from my *lvikao* and taking another long sip. . . . It's so creamy and delicately sweet, so rich with spices. "I would've liked to stay in that dome. Imagine the view from up there!"

Aeson looks at me with amusement. "Oh, but we *are* staying there tonight. I've made the reservation some time ago, and paid a very large, undisclosed sum to their visitors office to expedite our stay—at a moment's notice."

"Oh!" I exclaim with a smile. "Aeson, *thank* you!"

"But of course." He grins back at me. "And don't worry about the stairs. There's an external elevator that has been retrofitted for those unable to climb, that will take us all the way to the top."

"Wait, what?" I set down my mug, and lift my brows, giving *im amrevu* a somewhat dirty look. "What makes you think that I am *unable* to climb, that I don't want to walk up those ancient stairs like everyone else?"

Aeson stops chewing, while his eyes continue to sparkle with amused energy. "Well," he says carefully (yes, my Imperial Husband knows me well enough to be careful), "I was thinking of you straining yourself, and the baby—"

"Aeson!" I narrow my eyes at him in mock anger.

"All right, all right," he says, smiling at me. "But please promise me you will not overexert yourself."

"Of course I won't," I tell him, picking up my *lvikao* mug again and swirling it to watch the creamy contents go around.

"You won't what? Won't promise or won't overexert?" Aeson persists, watching me with bright, animated eyes.

I make a silly noise. "Take a guess! But no, seriously. We'll walk ridiculously slow, like decrepit people, and I will rest when needed."

"And if at any point you find it's too much, we will take the elevator the rest of the way," he says. "It is accessible from every landing, and there will be at least ten landings for you to change your mind as we climb."

"Fine. As long as *you*, mister, don't suddenly decide to carry me up those remaining stairs. Promise!"

"I think we have reached an understanding. I promise, you will not be treated as luggage." He looks at me, keeping his mouth very controlled to resist laughter. "Very precious luggage."

"We have," I say. "No hauling my precious heavy ass up the stairs. Else I will show you a terrifying thing or two in bed tonight, my Imperial Sovereign. You'll be sorry!" And I wiggle my brows meaningfully.

"I'm duly scared," he says, the corners of his lips shaking. "I am also very aroused. . . ."

"Aeson!" I reach across the table and swat his upper arm (so wonderfully hard and muscular that I can't help but pause to linger, allowing my fingers to caress him).

WE FINISH up our meal just as the view outside starts fading, in the growing dusk, to the deep teal shade of Atlantean twilight. And the stars come out far overhead where the evening has transformed to full lapis lazuli night.

The glory of the Atlantean sky replete with a trillion stars is a sight that never ceases to amaze me. . . .

"Too bad we're going to miss most of the natural light," I say, taking Aeson's hand to steady myself.

"Not to worry. Tomorrow morning will be bright when we descend. You'll see anything you might've missed on the way up. Besides, the Lighthouse interior and the stairs are well illuminated—since being a source of light is its main purpose."

We head outside, down the gentle ramp of the *depet*, and take our first steps onto the powdery sand and rock section of the beach.

It occurs to me, we're in Eos-Heket.

And it's cold!

I'm glad I wore a warm hooded cape over my regular clothing, upon Aeson's insistence. The crisp air engulfs us, and the evening breeze is strong, tugging immediately at my velvety hood. It finds its way inside, sliding in chill gusts along the nape of my neck, my face, and makes me wrap my hood closer.

Aeson squeezes my hand with his warm grip, and pulls me gently, helping me navigate the occasional larger stones. He too wears an elegant long coat over his normal jacket attire.

We approach the first service building, well-lit with golden orange orb light. I glance behind me and note that Imperial guards are accompanying us on this particular excursion. Among them is my own personal guard unit, including Tuar

Momet, looking serious and alert, since constant vigilance on my behalf is his responsibility. Finally, there are also several servants carrying luggage for our overnight stay. I dearly hope the burdened servants at least will take the Lighthouse elevator for their own sakes and leave us to ourselves during the climb. . . .

At the reception entrance of the building, we are greeted by two local officials, who stand up very straight and then bow before Aeson and me. They speak a slightly accented version of *Atlanteo* as they welcome us to the "unique heritage landmark that is the Ancient Hebu Lighthouse."

"The suite is ready for your stay, Sovereign of Imperial *Atlantida* and Sovereign Lady," the first of them says, bowing again. "Anything you require before your ascent? Refreshments, maybe?"

"No, just the keys," Aeson says with a light smile at me.

"Of course," the man replies, offering up a small card key on an ornate gilded tray etched with insignias in the shape of the Lighthouse tower. There is also a small, flattened disk-shaped device lying beside it.

"With our compliments, your automated tour guide," the man elaborates, pointing to the disk. "It contains the full library of antiquities, and will answer any of your questions along the way about the history of this landmark. Simply tap it and ask."

"Oh, how fun," I say.

"If you prefer, you can engage it for a formal tour, for the entirety of your ascent experience. Just toss it in the air after keying it with a standard tone. The automatic tour program will activate immediately, commenting on your exact location surroundings, and it will continue to respond to any of your verbal commands."

Aeson takes the key and hands me the tour guide disk.

"Please do watch your steps and tread carefully," the second official speaks up. "The stone stairs are somewhat steep in places and slippery from centuries of use."

"Thank you for the warning," Aeson replies, and glances at me meaningfully, raising one brow.

"Understood, thank you." I nod, holding the tour guide disk in my hand.

The officials incline their heads again. Then we all proceed from the service building toward the grand stone Lighthouse, situated approximately five hundred feet from us in the center of the clearing, towering endlessly over everything and fading into the mostly darkened sky. Only the crystal dome on the very top shines with impossible light, like a distant polar star. Meanwhile, the last remnant of Hel's setting glow seeps over the cliffs on the western horizon.

THE OLD WOODEN doors are opened before us, with an ominous creak of metal scraping against wood and stone. At once, orb illumination blooms forth, warming the interior with gold, and the ancient walls encrusted with coarse stones reveal themselves in a sudden flood of pallor.

I start to go inside, but Aeson hesitates at the entrance and gently takes my hand to hold me back.

"What?" I glance back at him.

But *im amrevu* smiles with sudden mischief, and beckons me back with one finger. "Wait. Before we go in, come back this way, and stand over here," he tells me, pointing to a spot several paces away, at the foot of the tower.

"What's going on?" I ask, obeying him out of curiosity.

Aeson continues to smile and then nods to the local officials who appear to wait for his command.

"Gwen, look up," Aeson says, pulling me against him and making me glance upward.

I lean back against his hard chest and throw my head back to stare up at the lofty radiant dome far overhead. "It is very beautiful."

We pause this way for several heartbeats. Just then, the last glimmer of sunset fades completely from the western sky.

Night is here.

And in that exact instant, something miraculous happens. The exterior stones of the tower begin to *glow*.

It is almost imperceptible at first, but within moments the glow turns brighter . . . and brighter.

"Oh, wow . . ." I whisper.

"Keep looking," Aeson tells me. "Orichalcum glow takes at least several daydreams to fully manifest itself."

"How is this possible?"

And then I remember the glowing symbols revealed on the pyramid stones during Stage Two of the Games of the Atlantis Grail.

"The entire Lighthouse has been keyed and programmed with an antique variant of the heating command," Aeson says. "The tower—all of it, not just the dome on the top—has to be clearly seen for many *mag-heitars* from the sea. It's been this way for centuries, in order to give the sailors a true vertical line of perspective in this long, narrow inlet of the sea."

"Truly amazing." I continue to look up, and now the tower is blazing, every exterior stone aglow, having turned into a distinctive bright obelisk silhouetted starkly against the night.

Now that it's all lit up, I can see its outlines better. From this close vantage, the structure of the tower appears roughly circular, approximately a hundred feet in diameter, slightly wider at the base nearest the ground, as far as I can tell. And then it rises and rises, barely narrowing and tapering off into the crystal dome portion somewhere up there. The dome looks so tiny, the size of an orange, from the ground.

"Let's walk around and see the whole of it before we enter."

Aeson nudges me with satisfaction, bringing me out of my reverie.

And we begin to walk the circumference of the ancient stones, discovering that the tower is indeed round. Meanwhile the retinue of our guards and the locals follow us at a polite distance of about ten steps.

"Is it all solid orichalcum?" I ask, peering at the glowing stones up-close, feeling a slight emanation of heat, and noting the familiar specks of fool's gold sparkling fiercely among the otherwise slate-grey surfaces. Those sparkles are a telltale sign of orichalcum—something I know quite well, by now.

"A combination of orichalcum, limestone and granite," Aeson replies. "The stones are composite. Even the ancients didn't have that much pure orichalcum on hand."

When we come back to the doors again, having circled the whole building, I pause, continuing to stare upward with genuine wonder at the immensity and sheer number of stones stacked on top of each other. Each crudely rectangular piece is two to three feet across.

There must be so much ancient Earth orichalcum here. . . .

Aeson touches me gently. "Now we can go inside."

"Thank you again," I whisper softly to *im amrevu*.

And we proceed inside the Hebu Lighthouse.

THE INTERIOR CONSISTS of a small landing, gently glowing walls, ceiling—everything wrought of coarse, faintly luminescent stone, except for the floor—with a rather narrow corkscrew staircase immediately before us. These indoor stones don't appear to be as bright as the ones on the exterior. However, they still exude a faint, warm, "fairy light" pallor, just enough to dispel complete darkness and soften it into permanent twilight. As for the main light sources, recessed alcoves are carved in the walls every few feet, with modern orbs installed, providing good lighting for the stairs.

Before we start our climb, four Imperial guards step forward and begin to walk quickly ahead of us up the stairs. In moments they disappear around the curve of the stairwell, and only the sound of their rapid footfalls continues to echo on the stones, eventually receding overhead.

"It's safety protocol," Aeson tells me quietly, seeing my surprised look. "The Imperator must be confined within a safe perimeter at all times in foreign territory. They must go before us and check for issues and secure all landings along the way. Give them a few moments to do their job."

And so, we pause briefly, waiting.

"All right, let's go," Aeson says with a light smile.

And we begin our climb. Not too far behind us, the rest of the Imperial guards follow.

THE STAIRS ARE DEFINITELY STEEP. Each step requires additional effort from me, something which I didn't quite expect. Also, there's barely enough room across for two people to stand next to each other, unless we want to bump elbows. It might make better sense if one of us takes the stairs ahead of the other. . . .

No, this isn't going to be an easy climb.

But, hell if I'm going to wimp out now, at the very beginning of this ordeal.

"Grab my hand." Aeson climbs effortlessly next to me, watching me take each step with super-focused effort.

"I'm fine." I shake my head, trying not to breathe loudly at this early juncture. I keep my expression composed and full of gravity.

Talking about gravity. . . . Ugh.

That's something else I forgot—that we're on Atlantis, and

the gravity of this planet is unpleasantly greater than Earth's. My family and I've grown generally accustomed to it over the months, but now and then, especially now that I'm pregnant, it really makes itself felt.

The corkscrew stairwell curves endlessly upward, ahead of us. I stare at each slightly bumpy, uneven, but well-polished stair, carefully placing one foot forward at each step, so as not to twist my ankles.

How many thousands of people climbed these stairs over the millennia, polishing the stones to such smoothness? And now, here I am, walking in their footsteps.

I no longer bother to cover up the fact that I'm breathing hard, and we haven't even reached the first landing. But I am moving just ahead of Aeson, not letting him see me *lag behind*.

"Want to stop for a moment?" Aeson asks me. His tone is gentle.

"Yes," I reply breathlessly. "But only because I want to turn on the tour guide."

We stop.

I stand, gathering my breath for the keying command. Then I raise one hand before me, open my palm, and sing the three notes of the keying sequence, F-A-C, at the orichalcum disk. Lurching in my palm, it comes alive with a small blue light, so I toss the disk into the air.

"Begin the guided tour of the Ancient Hebu Lighthouse," I command it. "If possible, please speak English."

The automated tour guide responds immediately, in a pleasant gender-neutral voice with a reasonably fair pronunciation of the English language. "You are on the ninety-third stair of the staircase of the Pharos, also known as the Hebu Lighthouse, fully reassembled in Eos-Heket, under the auspices of the House Urartumi, in the Year Four after Landing. Would you like to hear more?"

"Yes, please." I resume my climb.

The little disk, hovering noiselessly about a foot in front of my face, starts moving in tandem with my own motion.

And it launches the ancient history lesson, full of amazing facts and sometimes ridiculous, pedantic details and commentary. Some of it could be due to an inaccurate English translation from the Heketi language, or possibly random cultural differences.

I glance behind me periodically, rolling my eyes at some of the particularly super-weird tidbits, and see Aeson laughing.

CHAPTER 11

W e continue to climb the staircase to the first landing, where Aeson insists we stop to rest for a bit. The claustrophobic monotony of the otherwise windowless walls and regularly spaced light orb niches that accompanied our climb up to this point is, finally broken.

First, a strong draft signals the landing up ahead, then a blast of chill air hits us. The landing has three square windows in the curving stone wall—three openings to the outside world that offer a panoramic view of the star-filled *niktos* darkness outside, and permit wind to circulate freely throughout the tower. There is also a small, narrow door—rather modern looking—which, according to Aeson, is for elevator access.

"Elevator?" Aeson points casually to the door, but I shake my head.

"Nope. I want to keep going."

"Very well," he says with a smile.

And we continue up the next flight of stairs.

· · ·

". . . The lovers were separated and forced to climb the stairs on their own, never knowing where their beloved was, until the young nobleman collapsed on stair 387, only a few steps away from the second landing where his bride waited for him in vain. She waited until nightfall, and when he never showed, she flung herself from the central window of the landing and fell to her death, like a flightless *igunbua* bird that has only rudimentary wings. You are presently near the spot where the young man died on the stairs in the Year 204. His name and the name of his beloved are not recorded in history, but their ghosts are said to walk on the second landing exactly when Amrevet rises to fill the view from the central window, which happens during Green Season between first and third hour of Ra. . . ."

The digital tour guide continues regaling us with fascinating and strange bits of historical lore, just as we arrive on top of the second landing. Here, the fresh air and wind sweeps around us once again.

I huff my way up the last stair and stand on the landing, breathing loudly, with my back resting against the wall.

Aeson comes up right behind me, looking at me with concern.

"Second landing," I announce flippantly, with a smile—after a few heartbeats, after regaining my ability to speak. "Only eight more to go."

"Gwen. . . ." He places his hands on both my shoulders, holding me firmly before him. "You're a badass Games Champion. You know you don't have to prove anything to me or to anyone."

"I know," I say softly, looking up into his eyes. "But I have something to prove to myself."

"Okay."

"All right." I smile again, as my breathing slows to a more reasonable level. "Now, let's keep going."

"As you wish. . . ."

• • •

". . . The Blue Season snowfall of the Year 1209, coupled with the powerful storm winds, was so excessive that snowdrifts accumulated on every landing, in some cases blocking the stairs. Access to the third landing, in particular, was blocked completely by snow, and Lighthouse ground staff were sent to remove it, in order to make way for the Keepers of the Lighthouse and their Acolytes to be able to ascend all the way to the crystal dome, and perform regular maintenance of the Flame inside. . . ."

"Ah . . . so there's . . . a Flame . . ." I manage to utter between difficult breaths, while taking measured, slow steps. We're somewhere in the middle of the third flight, halfway to the third landing. "Obviously . . . there must be a Flame," I echo myself.

It's a lighthouse after all, so there has to be a light. What a dumb thing to forget.

And then something else obvious occurs to me, so I voice my thoughts. "Aeson, where will we be exactly? If there's a . . . big Flame up there, where will we stay?"

"Hm-m-m," Aeson makes a sound, moving right behind me. But before he can formulate a reply, our digital guide pauses its current narrative to answer my question.

"The Flame of the Pharos in its original colony form—as it had been ignited immediately after reassembly here on Eos-Heket—is no longer being utilized," the tour guide explains.

"Oh, really?" I pause my stride halfway between two stairs. "What happened? Please elaborate."

"After 9766 years of shining without interruption, the source of the Flame has been compromised and is no longer available to us, as of earlier this year. The Flame was permanently extinguished during Red Season of the Year 9771, at the time of the global alien conflict."

"This year? Okay, weird. Why? Who was responsible?" I ask, climbing the next step.

"The individual ultimately responsible was an Earth refugee and current Archaeona Imperatris of Imperial *Atlantida*, Gwenevere Kassiopei."

"What?" Frowning, I stop, and my mouth parts.

From a lower step, Aeson looks up at me curiously, and raises his brows, then smiles lightly.

"What in the world do you mean? That's *me!* I'm Gwenevere Kassiopei!"

The tour guide does not miss a heartbeat. "Welcome, Gwenevere Kassiopei, it is a pleasure to have you on this guided tour. You were responsible for the events described because you were responsible for the global liberation of the *pegasei*."

"The *pegasei*? Yes, but what does it have to do with—"

And then it hits me.

"The Flame—it was a flock of *pegasei!* They were somehow imprisoned in that crystal dome!" I say in wonder.

"That is correct," the guide replies, hovering before my face like an exotic insect. "The *pegasei* were released from their orb containment, and for the first time in known history the Lighthouse went dark. It remained thus for almost a week until a new illumination method was implemented."

"Oh my God . . ." I whisper. A weird sense of wonder strikes me, and my skin prickles with goosebumps.

I take a deep breath, while my temples continue to pound with elevated effort caused by the climb, and now—an additional sense of awe.

My actions during the apocalyptic events of the previous months had so many repercussions. . . . So many tendrils of cause and effect, so many concentric circles moving outward into the universe. *I know that.* But for some reason, this small detail really brings it home for me, yet again.

And so, I think and breathe. Then I lift my foot and take the next step.

THE CLIMB BECOMES a hypnotic labor of breathe-step-exhale, breathe-step-exhale, occasional stop, sit a few moments on the stairs, then continue. . . . By the time we reach the seventh landing, all while accompanied by the tour guide's narration of amazing historical facts, my head is spinning with exhaustion. I'm so lightheaded that I am ready to fly. . . .

"Gwen," Aeson tries again, his own breathing slightly elevated. "I'm pretty worn out myself. How about we take the elevator the rest of the way?"

Leaning against the wall, practically hugging it with my back, I stare at *im amrevu*. "Aeson," I whisper. "I'm sorry. Maybe you should just take the elevator without me? I don't want to make you do something like this just because of me. . . . But for some reason—for some wild reason I must finish this climb. I don't know why, but it's become a compulsion. I'm probably crazy. Maybe the baby hormones are kicking in and messing with me in a weird way. But I *have to* keep going."

"All right." Aeson leans closer to touch my clammy forehead. "But you know I'm not leaving you. We keep going—together."

"I knew you were going to say that—my beautiful, beloved jerk." I smile up at him.

We rest for a few daydreams, sitting down on the top stair of the landing, while the cold *niktos* wind blows around us. We sit side by side, and I rest my head against his solid, hard chest, and soon enough he wraps his strong arms around me.

"You know," I say softly. "I could focus very, very hard right now, and maybe, just maybe, you and I—we would simply be up there, on top of the Lighthouse . . . in a blink."

"You mean . . . *Starlight*?"

"Yes."

And then I chuckle and shake my head. "Except, now I'm being an idiot. I've never been there before, so I couldn't visualize our destination. . . . Never mind, my head is all woozy right now. Ignore what I just said, this is nonsense."

Aeson silently rubs the back of my neck in reply.

Starlight. . . .

I haven't used *Starlight* as a means of travel ever since my last demonstration to the various scientific authorities, many months ago. Especially not since my pregnancy advanced to the point where I couldn't risk endangering the child growing inside me. I've no idea what instantaneous *Starlight* travel might do to a baby. The whole thing is just . . . insanity.

So, yeah, no *Starlight*, and especially not now.

We continue resting a while longer (meanwhile, giving the Imperial guards a break also, somewhere ahead and behind us), then get up and continue the climb.

"CONGRATULATIONS! Before you are the final ten stairs of the ascent to the crystal dome," the tour guide says, hovering about ten inches away from my nose. "It is customary to recite the words of gratitude to the gods of sky, land, and sea, as you go up the final steps to the tenth and final landing at the top of the Pharos, also known as the Ancient Hebu Lighthouse. Would you like to hear the words of the Gratitude Prayer?"

Pausing my mechanical climb, I gasp out a faint reply, summoning my last breath. "Yes . . . please."

And the tour guide complies:

> Thank you, my feet, and the gods beneath
> who uphold me.
> Thank you, my lungs, and the gods of the
> air who fill me.

Thank you, my eyes, and the gods of the
    stars who guide me.
Thank you, my heart, and the gods of the
    music who drive me.
Foundation, path, destination, desire.
I breathe and give you back your light.

"Ah . . . I know this prayer," Aeson says softly, coming up behind me. "Except, we in *Atlantida* call it the Gratitude Song. It's taught to children in school."

"I really like it," I say. "Let's honor this tradition. . . . Go ahead and recite the words, since you know them, and . . . and I will repeat them with you."

"Gladly," my Imperial Husband says, taking my hand and stepping up next to me for a moment, so we end up squeezed together on the same narrow step. "Ready?"

We smile at one another—exhausted but apparently both of us feeling a peculiar high that is naturally produced by strenuous physical exertion. And then Aeson intentionally falls back again, letting me climb ahead on my own, while we remain linked by our words, spoken in unison—the words of Gratitude —as we climb the last ten stairs.

"We did it!" I announce with my last breath, after awkwardly echoing the Gratitude Prayer or Song or whatever it is, pausing briefly on the fifth stair, because it has gotten visibly brighter up ahead, and in just a moment my head will emerge onto the final landing. . . .

"No. *You* did it." Aeson's voice comes proudly from behind me.

"Well, I . . . can't believe . . . *I* did it!"

I whisper and giggle in exhaustion. Just then, I feel Aeson put his hand on my derriere—first slapping it lightly and then pushing me up by my rear end, ever-so-gently but firmly— helping me as I take the last stair, without any other supports to hold on to, emerging into . . . *wonder.*

The stairs end, and we arrive. Unlike the other landings, there is no welcoming wind. It is also still and quiet.

We are *here. . . .*

The view of the tenth landing is revealed before us, together with a gradual and then suddenly blazing golden radiance all around us.

The light comes from an unspecified source. As I blink to accustom my eyes, I realize that we are within a great glass dome rising over a perfectly circular floor space of polished stone. At its widest circumference, the enclosed space is the size of a large chamber.

The cupola of the dome encasing us is seamless glass alloy, with no visible supports, surrounding the perimeter of the floor. It looks almost unreal, fragile, like the upper hemisphere of a giant frozen bubble with an iridescent surface. And beyond it, from every direction, stretches the grand, starlit, Atlantean *niktos* sky.

We are surrounded by nothing but night and sky in this fragile bubble of glass. . . .

The stairwell from which we've just emerged is a small rectangular opening in the floor, off to the side, and away from the center.

In the middle of the chamber is an upraised stone dais, also a perfect circle, about twelve feet in diameter. It contains . . . a ceramic planter pot. Just a simple round bowl filled with colorful flowers growing from the soil.

"Oh," I say. "How unusual! Flowers!"

"Yes." Aeson squeezes my hand lightly, and there's a mischievous expression on his face. "They are a very recent addition. That's where the Flame used to be—*pegasei* encased in a very large orb, resting in the center of that round stone altar."

My eyes widen. "So it wasn't a planter before? I see!"

"No, it wasn't. This bowl is the remnant of the original stone holder for the quantum orb. Once the *pegasei* were released and the orb containment dissolved, they decided to add soil and make it a living, decorative centerpiece. A good way to utilize the vacant space."

"How cool!" I take a few steps toward the vase filled with greenery—indigo, mauve, white, blood-red scarlet, and cream flowers, some of them possibly Earth roses. "What about the replacement Flame? What's the new source of all this light?"

The little tour guide disk, still following me, speaks up: "Currently, a different method is utilized to light the crystal dome. The surface of the dome is a special glass alloy treated with orichalcum and containing solar nano-light technology. The dome itself shines brightly on the outside, but on the inside, it is merely a soft glow. During the day the surface of the dome charges itself for the night illumination."

"So, in a sense, it's not unlike what the *pegasei* did when they fed on Hel's light," Aeson says.

In that moment, I see the strange sight of several Imperial guards literally rising from the floor on the opposite side of the dome chamber. I stare in initial amazement, but then realize they are coming up from another recessed staircase, just as we did.

These are the same Imperial guards who had gone before us to secure the way. They approach Aeson and explain politely that the guest chambers below are now cleared and secured for our use.

"Thank you," Aeson tells them. "You are now dismissed for the night."

The guards salute both of us then head out, this time using the same staircase by which we arrived.

After they're gone, I turn to Aeson with a tired but silly smile. "Well, that answers two of my questions. I was wondering where they had disappeared to, and also wondering where we are actually sleeping."

"Not underneath the vase of flowers?" Aeson retorts mischievously.

"Well, we *could*," I say. "I'm kind of ready to collapse anywhere, and this shiny stone floor looks pretty good, right about now."

"Fear not, *im amrevu*." Aeson takes me by the hand. "There's a small but comfortable suite of rooms below us. Come!"

"The staircase portion of your guided tour is completed," the little hovering disk tells me just then. "Would you like to hear the history of the crystal dome?"

"How about later," I say with a smile. "Please pause the tour."

And the little disk guide complies, coming to rest on my open palm and growing silent in hibernation mode.

WE GO DOWN that other little opening in the floor and descend the staircase. Normally this opening is closed off with a sliding hatch—a kind of discreet trapdoor—that can be unlocked or locked for privacy with the card key that Aeson received from the Lighthouse officials. In our case, it was left unlocked for the Imperial guards to do their initial safety inspection of our quarters.

This time, Aeson leads the way, likely so that he can catch me as I tumble down the stairs (which I almost do). Good thing he's there to grasp me in his strong arms. There are only about ten stairs, and we find ourselves in a compact but modern, well-furnished suite. There's a large bed with many pillows, a comfortable sofa and chairs, a table and, further down a small corridor, an adjacent luxury bathroom with a full tub and shower.

"This is amazing!" I exclaim, still holding onto Aeson. "We have a real bed!"

He chuckles. "Of course. And there's even a *niktos* meal."

The table, I realize, has several covered dishes, ready for us. It's probably been delivered by elevator while we were still climbing, timed very well for our arrival.

"All that's missing is a cat!" I laugh, semi-collapsing on the nearest overstuffed chair. "I wonder how Ohri is doing without us."

"He is very likely sleeping on our bed, having eaten and eliminated properly." Aeson walks up to the table and lifts the cover from one of the dishes. At once a delicious aroma of savory, spicy food assails us, and there is fresh steam rising from the dish with its colorful ingredients. "Still hot. Looks good. I like Heketi food, especially their pickled *wotimi* soup. It's similar to Earth garlic, but without the excessive stench."

"Oh, I'm starving!" I say, almost in surprise, remembering the needs of my stomach.

"Yes, you are. And so is the baby. So, first we eat!"

I don't need to be told twice.

"WHAT KIND OF ROOM IS THIS?" I ask, as I wash up in the bathroom before our meal, running the water in an elegant rose stone sink. "Did the Lighthouse Keepers use these quarters?"

"Yes," Aeson says, toweling off his face after rinsing the fine sweat from his forehead. "Although, they enlarged the area and retrofitted it into a guest suite. The original chamber was tiny, just enough room for a sleeping bunk and an elimination area. And now this is a very exclusive place, with people paying large sums to stay here, while the Lighthouse Keepers stay in the settlement below. Since everything up here is automated tech, there is little for them to do, actually."

"No need to look after *pegasei* anymore."

"Right. They merely check the integrity of the dome glass periodically."

We return to the main room and fall upon our feast.

And oh my, but Heketi food is indeed very good! Light and creamy dishes, with just enough spice to be fragrant but not overpowering like Deshi food (which I found to be a little too much, if I'm honest).

My tiredness comes over me, and I feel the warmth of the food fill me with a soporific delight, so I wolf it down until I'm stuffed. Aeson is not far behind, his own appetite ravenous after our epic climbing exercise.

Afterwards, we both simply plop on top of the bed, still wearing all our clothing except for the outer coats, and close our eyes in perfect satiation. I've no idea when, but we must've both gone directly to sleep.

WHEN I WAKE UP, it's the middle of the night, according to the small timepiece on the side table. The lights in the bedroom have dimmed gently, and Aeson is asleep just as he was, lying unmoving at my side, his deep breathing audible.

Lord, but he must've been so terribly tired too, after that climb. Poor Aeson, I forced him to do this insane climb because of me. And all those poor guards too. I hope they're all getting a good rest, at least. . . .

Random, guilty thoughts come into my head. I shift slightly, stare up at the somewhat boring low ceiling (compared to the rest of the décor), then get up with some effort, but without any sound. My feet ache as I tiptoe to the bathroom to empty my bladder.

When I return to bed, Aeson is awake. He yawns, stretches, and smiles at me.

"It's the third hour of Ra," I say, stroking his cheek. "We should get to bed for real."

"We should." He rises on his elbows. "But now is the perfect time to go up and look through the crystal dome at the sky."

"Okay," I say softly. "We can sleep more later."

WE LEAVE our quarters and climb up to the dome landing, and oh . . . the moons are rising! I hadn't realized what was missing from the sky earlier, but now the night is almost as bright as daylight, because the huge lavender disk of Amrevet fills most of the sky view on one side, like a floating orb outside the dome glass.

On the opposite end, I see tiny silver Pegasus near zenith, and far below it, the upper portion of the setting white-and-mauve disk of Arlenari, formerly known as the Ghost Moon. Only Mar-Yan is still out of sight.

We stand at the edge of the dome glass and stare, both of us. . . . A soft, dreamy smile comes to Aeson's face. And then he turns to me and says quickly. "Stay here. I'll be right back."

My Imperial Husband heads back down the stairs to our guest suite. Moments later he emerges again, carrying a thick blanket and several pillows. "Let's lie down here for a while and look up. The *niktos* sky is amazing here, not to be missed."

"Good idea," I say.

Together we spread the blanket up on the dais near the centerpiece of flowers, and rest the pillows against the edge of the stone bowl. And then we crouch down and make ourselves comfortable on the blanket that serves us as a thin mattress.

I lower my head in the crook of Aeson's left arm, tuck a pillow under me, fluff up the one underneath Aeson's head, and we both just lie back and stare overhead into star-filled infinity.

"See that?" Aeson points. "Pegasus is moving between several bright, jagged stars."

"Yes, I see."

"That's the Jaw. These stars form the Jaw of the Air Sebeku."

"The crocodile!" I say.

A few moments later, I point to a different bright spot in the sky that has another interesting configuration of stars, four large ones forming a cross. "And what's that?"

"Ice Astroctadra," Aeson replies.

"And that?" I single out a crescent-curve of prominent stars with one brightest star in the center.

"Quantum Depet."

"Oh yeah . . . I see the boat shape."

We continue this way for the next few daydreams, or maybe a quarter hour, while Aeson identifies the various constellations of the Atlantean Zodiac.

And then suddenly, Aeson's hand squeezes my wrist. "There! There it is!" he says with a soft smile.

"What?"

And then I see it. The entire lower portion of the sky at the edges of the dome is emanating a strange teal and green *warping glow*—a numinous radiance which almost *moves* (but maybe not?) like a mirage, reminding me of something. . . .

Aurora borealis. Known on Earth as the Northern Lights.

"Oh!" I whisper. "I see it!"

"I was really hoping we would get to see them tonight," Aeson says with pleasure. "We call them the *nemsetara*—Polar Flood Skies. The planetary magnetic field dances brightly, being so far north, near the pole."

"I love it!" I say, "Just like on Earth."

"The magnetic field of Atlantis is even more robust, which is a good thing. It protects us better from cosmic radiation."

"And it does it beautifully."

We grow silent, simply gazing upward.

Periodically Aeson points out celestial objects in the sky and tells me curiosities and random stuff . . . and silly things from his childhood . . . and just cute little things *about himself.*

Much of what he tells me is rambling, sometimes ridiculous, spoken in a boyish, innocent tone of voice. And so, I listen with wonder, keeping my cheek pressed against his chest.

Hearing all of it makes my heart ache, for some reason. There's a feeling so overpowering that it has to be love. . . .

The moons creep across the sky softly, shifting their positions.

At some point, I place one hand on Aeson's chest and caress it slowly through the fine cloth of his shirt. Then I start unbuttoning it.

"M-m-m," he says, his lashes flickering with relaxation.

"Thank you," I whisper. "For bringing me *here*."

And then my fingers slide down his naked chest. When I reach the V-shape of his taut abdomen, my fingers wander lower and I begin undoing his pants.

Aeson makes a deep sound, as I rub my hand rhythmically against the growing bulge in his crotch, undo the final clasps, and release him. His instantly hard dick pulses with heat and fills my hands, and my husband's breathing intensifies.

"Ah . . . Gwen," he groans thickly. "Yes. . . ."

"You like that?" I ask, my voice going low and wicked. And I tug at the Big Boy, making him groan again.

"*Varqood* me," he commands in his deep baritone, his breath coming harshly.

He puts one heavy hand at the back of my neck, pulling me closer, his strong fingers digging at my scalp. Then he throws his head back and shuts his eyes against the moon-and-star-filled night, parting his lips.

I make an even more wicked sound, then lower my face to lick his balls, while my skillful fingers continue to work the length of the Imperial *serpent*.

Somewhere overhead, a different serpent, the Gravity Uraeus, casts its flickering light upon us. Just a few heartbeats later, like a blazing comet, Aeson Kassiopei, Archaeon Imperator of *Atlantida, im vuchusei amrevu,* comes hot in my mouth.

CHAPTER 12

I awake with white light incinerating my eyelids, to a fiercely blazing dawn. . . .

Aeson and I have once again fallen asleep outside of our designated bed—in the observation area on top of the blanket, right where we were—and never even made it to the nice guest bedroom below. Who knows when it happened? We were wallowing in such a state of sweet lassitude, long into the *nemsetara*-lit starry night. Because what followed was even more sexy intimacy in which we engaged for quite some time, thoroughly staining the blanket underneath us.

All I remember now is that, after he orgasmed from my oral ministrations, Aeson pulled me up to straddle his face, so that he could take his turn and lick me down *there*. . . .

Already very aroused from handling his big *varqooi* (as he calls his dick), I ended up on top of him, spread wide, with his strong hands supporting my hips from below while he ate me. Trembling with built-up tension, moaning, I climaxed almost immediately from the rhythmic suction pull of his lips upon my clit. . . . Then we swapped places, with him on top, and Aeson rode me hard until we both collapsed.

But, a mere daydream later, his *varqooi* was stiff as a rock again. . . .

Ah, my sweet, insatiable *amrevu*.

AND NOW, Hel is blasting its morning light at the crystal dome, and the light is amplified a thousandfold, it seems, and converted by the special glass into white fire. This is how the dome recharges itself for its nightly beacon duty.

"Aeson!" I squint, putting my hand over my eyes as I lie on my back, cradled against his naked chest, enjoying the feel of his warm strength enclosing me, our limbs entwined.

Meanwhile, *im amrevu* stirs around me, waking up with a deep, in-drawn breath and a yawn. He squeezes me to him, then narrows his eyes also.

"*Bashtooh*, that's really bright," he admits with a sleepy smile. "We never made it to bed. There's a good reason the bedroom is windowless and hidden below. This!"

"So crazy bright!" I agree, sitting up awkwardly on the blanket, and pushing a pillow out of the way.

Aeson immediately assists me and my pregnant belly, and we both stand up and stretch and try not to go blind in the impossible radiance all around us.

Seriously—right now, the dazzling brightness in this chamber is so strong that it's genuinely hard to see through the dome and get an inkling of the panoramic view outside.

Soupy white haze. . . . That's the entirety of the world out there.

"I think, the angle of Hel's sunrise striking the orichalcum coating of the dome makes it like this," my husband tells me as we gather our pillows and bedding and walk back down to the guest suite. "Once it's higher up in the sky, closer to zenith, the light becomes more manageable, and we'll get the perfect view of the land and sea all around."

We shower and clean up the usual intimate sticky stuff, then get dressed, and Aeson calls the Hebu Lighthouse visitor office and orders us *eos* bread to be brought up.

"Don't worry," he says, noticing my concerned expression. "They'll use the service elevator."

"Oh good." I plop down in a soft chair and let out a sigh, finding my legs and feet slightly sore this morning after yesterday's long climb. Not to mention, the place *between* my legs is sore from a different exercise entirely. "I would hate for anyone to have to carry heavy dishes up those thousand stairs, especially on my behalf."

Our meal arrives soon after, supposedly on an old-fashioned rolling service cart that remains on the nearest landing of the stairwell below. Meanwhile, the actual dishes are carried the final few steps up, on large trays, by two uniformed staff, a man and woman, who bow politely, then start setting our table. Delicious aromas fill the air, a bouquet of sweet and savory spices and hot, steaming *lvikao*.

As soon as the servants leave, also having removed last night's empty dishes, we consume our feast in comfortable silence. At some point I toss the tour guide gadget up in the air, letting it entertain us while we eat. As soon as it activates, I ask it a few historical questions.

"Why is this country called Eos-Heket?" I query, sipping amazingly delicious Heketi *lvikao* with unexpected notes of citrus and cinnamon from my hot mug, while Aeson watches me with amusement.

The guide lights up with colors, then the unit responds. "According to our earliest historical records, the name Eos-Heket comes from the ancient period soon after Landing. It combines two names, that of a woman called Eos and her companion Heket, either a man or a child. Legend has it, they flew across the sky, spanning the entire length and width of the land and defining the territorial boundaries that formed the eventual borders of our nation—borders that are used to this day. Another theory suggests that Eos originally referred to 'early' or 'dawn' or 'East,' the direction, and Heket referred to its opposite, 'late' or 'West,' and it simply meant our nation is immense and spans the entirety of the continent."

"Eos-Heket spans one half of the Upper Continent, at most," Aeson says in a bemused tone. "Closer to one third, actually."

I purse my lips in a smile. The tour guide flickers with colored light, as though digesting Aeson's commentary. And then, unperturbed, it continues: "A third theory claims that Eos-Heket is a variation on the name 'Hekatria,' an ancient divination game that uses a deck of symbolic image cards. It was originally utilized by priests of the goddess Hekatri to read and interpret human events, reveal hidden aspects of character, and guide future actions of rulers and commoners."

"Oooh, that should be fun!" I say. "I like the idea of Hekatria. Sounds like old Earth Tarot."

Aeson chuckles and picks up his own steaming mug. "I'll get you a deck. They are quite common on Atlantis, found in every trinket shop world-wide, not just in Eos-Heket. Some of them are rather artfully done. In fact, we can drop by the Lighthouse tourist gift shops on the ground level, before we leave, to see if they have any."

"Great," I say with a crafty expression. "I've an idea of what we can do with these cards. . . . Just you and me, playing late at night. Possibly naughty."

"I am almost afraid to ask, while I'm also very eager to find out," my husband replies with a very steady, very sensual look of his midnight-deep blue eyes.

WE WAIT for a couple of hours in the soothing, dimly illuminated interior of the guest suite for the light in the dome above to decrease to bearable levels. As usual, Aeson scans messages and other work-related stuff on his wrist unit. He also checks in with the captain of our *nubu depet* for a status update, including the well-being of our new cat Ohri, (which, he tells me, has just been fed, and has eliminated quite properly in its box).

Meanwhile, I call up the large Atlantean video screen from its recessed spot on one of the walls and watch the local programming on the multiple window feeds in the Heketi language—just for fun, to see if I can understand any of it. And nope, I don't. It's entirely different from *Atlanteo*, more guttural and a little throaty, with several unusual sounds that blend together "g," "gh," and "kh," with subtle differences.

However, in one of the feed windows I notice they are showing something about Earth, so I pause scrolling and enlarge focus on that window, letting it fill the entire screen. It's some kind of intergalactic video interview with an Earth official from the National Museum of China who is speaking in a heavily accented English (for the sake of the Atlanteans who are generally most familiar with English), and is using an agitated tone.

". . . No, we expect some kind of compensation—now, not later, *now*—for the loss of Chinese national treasure," the Chinese museum official says in a firm voice, then picks up a paper list and starts to read. "So much treasure, gone! You, *Atlantida rén*, you have the Neolithic jade dragons, the Han Dynasty bronze Hu vessel, the—"

"We are not *Atlantida*, and we don't," the interviewer from somewhere here on Atlantis replies in a bland voice, also in a strongly accented English, but with an entirely different accent. "You speak to Shuria. You understand? *Shuria!* We—not same thing! Imperial *Atlantida* is big, we are not big! We are across ocean! Our museum has Shuri national treasure, not your *chazuf* hoo vessel! Our records don't show anything like hoo vessel in Khur Museum inventory—"

"*Bú duì!*" The Chinese official breaks into Mandarin with a frown and shakes his head emphatically, then continues in English. "Incorrect! Not right! No! It says here, you, *somebody*, have bronze Hu, from Han period—"

I start giggling, and Aeson looks up from his wrist device with a smirk. "Museum interplanetary conflicts, again?" he asks, and raises one brow to glance at the officials yelling on-screen.

"Oh yeah," I reply with my own wiggle of brows. "Museum *wars*. It never ends. My Dad would just 'love' seeing this. He has very strong but also very complex and nuanced opinions about such long-term cultural appropriation."

"I can only imagine." Aeson shakes his head in amusement.

WE FINALLY VENTURE upstairs into the crystal dome. Hel is safely halfway up the sky, and the glass-like transparent material comprising the dome has absorbed most of its incredible light energy charge, so that we can safely see the world outside without going blind.

Aeson and I stand looking through that magic glass bubble at the impossible panorama of sky and land and sea, in all its aerial glory. From this distance, the long inlet stretch of Hebu Sea appears metallic grey fading into inky blue and then faint silver at the horizon, against the white sky. On both sides, land beyond the small beach rises into mauve cliffs with very little vegetation.

From the height of our vantage point, everything is tiny and delicate, as though etched in hair-thin lines of darkness over chalk pallor. The wind must be strong, coming in gusts out there, because what little vegetation there is, sways periodically from the onslaught of air. . . .

We gaze outward, mesmerized, for several long daydreams.

Until Aeson's wrist unit chimes with an incoming notification. He checks it and, apparently the captain of our *depet* has conveyed a formal invitation to us from the Honorable Kephasa Sewu, the Oratorat of Eos-Heket.

"Yes! We're going to Ushab!" I exclaim.

Aeson smiles. "The Oratorat can't wait to receive us."

AND SO, we leave the glorious crystal dome, and descend into the main access entrance stairwell, down the short flight of stairs from which we originally came, to the nearest landing. Here, we are joined by Imperial guards who must've been stationed on this landing all this time.

Yes, it's their job, but I always feel guilty, and give my own personal guard Tuar Momet a tiny, bashful smile which he returns in a no-nonsense, professional manner. Then, all of us pile into the roomy Lighthouse elevator, a modern high-tech addition to this antique landmark.

The exterior wall of the elevator is made of clear glass material, like the dome, so that we can see our rapid descent and viscerally experience the illusion of the ground rising up to swallow us.

Once outside, the morning wind hits us, crisp and invigorating. I stand back, squinting from the familiar glare of Hel, ready to put on my wraparound sunglasses. Briefly I look up at the towering Lighthouse with its now-distant crystal dome reaching for the clouds, almost disbelieving we were just up there . . . marveling yet again.

In that moment Aeson looks up also, and we share glances of wonder.

We walk to the tourist building, and Aeson returns the bedroom suite card key to the officials there—a key for that small sliding trapdoor for the bedroom suite that we never bothered to use, feeling no need to lock ourselves in.

"Gift shop?" I say with a playful smile, and my Imperial Husband nods.

There's a sensual, amused expression in his eyes as he watches me, and the tiniest movement at the corners of his lips. It's that familiar look that says, *I can't deny you anything.*

I'm definitely getting my Hekatria deck.

CHAPTER 13

The gift shops and other tourist establishments line up in a row on the main street of this small settlement. The buildings are old but not ancient, mostly no more than two floors, and a curious mixture of Hel-bleached cream stone bricks and brightly painted wood in shades of red, orange, and black. From what I can tell, having only a rudimentary familiarity with Atlantean architecture, these are much later additions compared to the venerable ancient landmark they surround.

The street below us is formed of the same mauve paving material that is found in major cities such as Poseidon in Imperial *Atlantida*, but it's only a narrow strip, stretching in parallel to the buildings. As soon as the buildings end, the ground turns to gravel and then rough stone in the distance.

The morning light of Hel streams brightly on this scene, and the street is mostly empty, except for one or two individuals loitering near doorways, who might be staff working in this complex.

"Where are the other tourists?" I whisper to Aeson with a silly smile.

"This is quite a remote area, and as far as I know, it doesn't get that many visitors, especially this time of year," he replies. "Also, since we're here, most people's reservations have been shifted to accommodate our Imperial stay."

"Even as far as walking in the street?"

"Very likely so."

"Oh dear," I mumble with a minor twinge of guilt. "We stayed up there in the dome, and none of these people were allowed to climb the stairs while we were there—right?"

"Right." Aeson chuckles. "Local Eos-Heket authorities decided to play it safe and restrict access to the area in general while we are here, and avoid any possible international incidents."

I squint in the morning glare, even with sunglasses on, shaking my head.

And then I see a curious looking sign over the front of the nearest building. It's a digital billboard, somewhat out of place here—modern and comparable to what I've seen on the streets in Poseidon. But what makes it unusual is that it is literally shaped like the silhouette of the Pharos, the Ancient Hebu Lighthouse structure, and it is pulsing with waves of light that travel up its tower form and then explode in rhythmic bursts of radiance from the dome shape at the apex.

The light flashes are so bright that they are noticeable even in the overwhelming glare of Hel.

"What's that?" I touch Aeson's arm and point.

"The trinket-filled place you've been searching for," *im amrevu* replies with amusement. "Gift shop, souvenir shop, visitor welcome center."

And we head directly for it.

WE STEP inside this Heketi establishment and find a true indoor marketplace. Not unlike Earth stores, the entire space is covered with colorful and shiny merchandise, tantalizingly arranged on shelves and rotating stands. There is so much garish stuff that I momentarily freeze, with my lips parted.

I see a uniformed woman toward the back, who must be the shopkeeper. She looks somewhat elderly, and wears a curious little hat that looks a bit like an old-fashioned Earth bonnet, but on a tiny scale, almost like a fascinator hat worn in Great Britain to formal events. This funny little hat is attached directly over her graying brown hair that's taken up in a bun on top of her head.

It's literally a *bun hat*.

I hold back a giggle, out of respect.

The shopkeeper woman sees us enter her establishment, and immediately hurries toward us. She bows neatly before Aeson and me, and says in heavily accented *Atlanteo*, "Welcome, Imperial Sovereign Lord and Lady, please enjoy and please buy our gifts! Gifts for you and for your family! Many gifts! Enjoy! Enjoy! Thank you!"

And without saying anything else, or waiting for our response, she bows again and retreats back to her little desk and what I assume is a checkout counter.

"Thank you," I mutter in her wake, and then see her sit down and proceed to ignore us. So much so, that I'm certain she is watching us like a hawk.

Apparently, this sales method is universal, on Earth and on Atlantis. Merchants and sales people who want to set at ease any potentially splurging customers and let them shop at leisure, know better than to hover. . . .

I take a deep breath and look at Aeson. "I have all those *iretar* in my credit account."

"You also have the entirety of the Imperial credit account at your disposal," Aeson adds, leaning down to speak near my ear, and I feel his warm breath tickle my cheek. "If you like, I can buy you this whole store. And the building which houses it." And he keeps his lips in a very tight, controlled line, holding back laughter. "But you probably don't want that."

"No-o-o-o," I say, patting him on the arm. "I *said*, I have my own *iretar*, mister. Let me use them."

His eyes fill with even more amusement, but my Imperial Husband says nothing, merely gestures me to the merchandise.

And so, I start browsing.

I've never been much of a shopper, but I do like to examine pretty, curious trinkets—especially alien ones, in this case. In such fun-filled curiosity shops I tend to zone out and stare closely at the little details, the play of light on sparkling shapes and surfaces, beautiful color combinations, while my mind floats away into a pleasant daydream. . . .

I have to admit, this place is wonderful.

There seems to be everything imaginable here—jeweled trinkets, Lighthouse mini-toys and souvenirs, dishes and drinkware, including beautiful chalices and grails. I walk the aisles and see elegant dolls dressed in intricate Heketi folk costumes, formed with loving details, like miniature people. There are fabric stuffed animals resembling gazelles and embroidered flying birds with iridescent wings, carved pieces of wood shaped like the Hebu Lighthouse and polished and painted in bright colors. Garlands of costume jewelry hang from branches of display trees, small electronic gadgets stamped or embossed with the iconic Lighthouse image sit in trays, and various unknown objects peek or sparkle at me.

As I move toward the back of the store, Aeson follows me casually, giving me space. He also periodically stops to examine items. Ahead, there are aisles with shelves of tourist and traveler media, both digital and print. There are antique-style classic Atlantean scrolls, and more Earth-like bound books—only with odd rounded pages shaped like the letter D.

"Are these books about Eos-Heket?" I ask Aeson, opening one of the rounded books to leaf through parchment-like, stiff pages filled with glossy illustrations and text in a foreign alphabet which I've never seen before.

Aeson glances at the volume I'm holding. "Yes, this one's a Heketi sightseeing book. Those images are popular historic landmarks, entertainment venues, and eateries, further south. Closer to Ushab, the capital city."

"I see." I set the book back down carefully, and continue browsing.

A FEW MORE STEPS IN the printed media aisle, and Aeson points out to me rows of stacked rectangular boxes. "You were looking for these," he says, picking up one of the small packs and turning it this and that way to show off gilded edges and corners and beautiful geometric designs with elegant flourishes. "These are Hekatria decks. Different themes and minor variations of design, but the idea is the same. Divination play."

"Ooh!" I exclaim with enthusiasm, and select one of the packs with particularly intricate imagery and beautiful earth tone colors, depicting curious symbols surrounded by curving vines. "I'll take this one."

"Good choice. This is a flora deck," my husband tells me. "It's based on plants and flowers."

"And this one," I say, taking a second one, with what appears to be celestial symbols.

"Hm-m-m, a star and moon deck." Aeson nods. "I think you'll really like this one."

"I can't wait." I run my fingers over the smooth surface of the dark-blue printed box which has an image of the night sky and is embossed with gilded stars and planets. "I hope it comes with instructions. Does it?"

"Usually, yes. There will be an insert or booklet. I'll translate for you."

"Perfect! And now I need a shopping basket—"

"Here, I'll carry them." Aeson simply takes both decks from me, freeing up my hands for more purchases.

We continue strolling through the store until we come to an aisle of items that literally stop me in my tracks.

My jaw drops and I laugh.

Rows and rows of phallic objects stand up to attention. They appear to be dildos, of every possible shape, pattern, and color, some of them even vaguely *shaped* like the Hebu Lighthouse. Interspersed with them are other items that I have no doubt are of a sexual nature. Penile rings and vaginal beads and nipple clamps and . . . cute little floggers. There are also bottles of creams and lubricants, packages of what must be condoms, or their Atlantean equivalent, and booklets with pictures of people in various intimate positions.

"Oh my God . . ." I say, placing my hand on Aeson's upper arm.

He stops and gives me one of his humorous looks, with one brow raised, and a smile barely twitching at the corners of his mouth.

"Is that—" I start to ask. "Are those sex things?"

"*Amrevet* toys, yes," my husband tells me with an amused, provocative expression. "They're rather common."

"Just like that? Out in the open, in a tourist gift shop?" I continue in silly amazement.

"Of course. Why not?" Aeson looks curiously at me. "Tourists have physical needs like anyone.

"Oh. . . ." I smile somewhat awkwardly. "So then, this store is not just a gift shop. It's kind of like an Earth drugstore."

I recall now that Atlanteans seem to have fewer hangups about nudity and sexuality than Earth natives.

I take a big breath and advance to stare at the rows of phalluses, growing like mushrooms on the shelves, some of them ridiculously huge and scary looking, others petite and flexible, others yet in cheerful colors.

"Wow, look at this one, Aeson," I whisper with embarrassment, then pick up the biggest cock wand which appears to be made of some silicone-like substance and is at least 12 inches long and as wide as my wrist. "This is elephant sized."

"Want to buy it?" he asks in all seriousness.

"Hell, no!" I exclaim. "This is scary big! I can't even imagine something like that fitting inside—"

Aeson just looks at me with amusement.

"Don't look at me like that!" I giggle. "Just having *you* inside can be a challenge, but this thing?"

"So—you say, I'm a challenge?" Aeson continues to watch me very intensely.

"No, that's not what I mean," I hurry to explain, lowering my voice to a whisper, so that the nosy shopkeeper in the back will have no chance of hearing me. "You're *fine*, but you *are* big! Really big, as it is! But this thing—that's a monster!"

Aeson chuckles, as I quickly put the giant dildo back in its spot. "No! Stay back!" I say again, addressing the dildo like a dog and wagging one finger at it.

Then I feel my husband's hand squeezing my ass.

It's a casual but lingering touch, but the look in his eyes is unmistakable.

"You should buy something else then," he says, looking at me languidly, and no longer smiling. "Something just for you."

He leans down to speak near my ear. "I want to *watch* you use it."

"Uhm, okay . . . are these just dildos that don't move, or are they vibrators?" I ask, feeling the heat of a flush rising in my cheeks, but also starting to get a little breathless. Honestly, I am still not that comfortable talking about these things, even after all this time.

"Some of these are. Similar to the electric gadgets you have on Earth." Aeson picks up one medium-sized cock, purple-colored with a pretty gold pattern on the base near the rather sizeable gilded balls. He turns over the base and shows me an on-off switch. "This one's not too big, and has a decent texture, so you should be able to enjoy it. This little nub is for additional clitoral stimulation."

"Shush! For God's sake, Aeson, I don't need this thing when I have you!" I say, turning bright red.

"I'll be happy to stimulate you all by myself, but I want you to enjoy it even more. That's why *amrevet* toys exist, to add fun," my Imperial Husband says, standing very close and brushing up against me from behind.

Suddenly I feel the Imperial *varqooi* poking my behind, despite all the layers of clothing between us.

"All right . . . let's just pay for all these and go back to the *depet*," I whisper, turning to look in his eyes. But you have to carry that vibrator for me and deal with the shop lady—"

Aeson laughs. "No problem."

He then walks the aisle, selects several more erotic items, including a cute little Lighthouse-shaped dildo with a blinking light attachment—even as I gape in embarrassment—then takes my hand possessively, pulling me after him.

Armed with *amrevet* toys and Hekatria decks, we head toward the check out.

CHAPTER 14

W e arrive at the back of the store, where the shopkeeper sits behind her desk, and Aeson unceremoniously unloads our purchases on the counter—I should say, mostly *his* purchases, because I swear, I had nothing to do with all those adult toys he grabbed from the shelves.

Lord, help me. . . . I'm dying of embarrassment.

The shopkeeper immediately looks up, giving us her full attention, then looks down at the merchandise. "Ah, good gifts, excellent selections!" she exclaims at once.

I feel my cheeks beginning to burn.

The woman starts picking up each item, checking the prices, and entering them in her register. She also makes comments about each one, to my utter mortification.

"You—Imperial Sovereign Lord and Lady, enjoy your *amrevet* bed tonight, eh? Very, very nice! This one—" she picks up a little lube jar that Aeson threw in there, and twists the lid slightly, then sniffs at it—"this one smells nice when you lick! Very tasty. This lubricating sauce—sweet like fruit!"

She turns to Aeson. "Young man, even Imperial young man, must please his wife, always."

Aeson looks down at the woman with a shadow of amusement. "Of course," he replies confidently.

The jerk! He's not even the least bit uncomfortable!

The shopkeeper turns to me. "And young woman—" Just then she notices my pregnant belly. "Ah! You are already carrying baby, good! Your first one?"

"Yes. . . . We are on our Amrevet Days," I say, gathering my courage.

"Ah, may all the gods of this world bless you and the little one, Imperial Sovereign Lady!" The woman begins smiling widely, and suddenly turns to the merchandise again, examining each item with a renewed level of scrutiny—indeed, an intensive, focused perusal. She picks up the purple dildo with the golden pattern, and turns it in her hand critically, then looks Aeson up and down.

What is happening here?

"Show me your hand," she says suddenly, unceremoniously tapping Aeson's arm.

"What?" My husband watches her curiously.

"Put it here, put your hand here!" the woman tells him in a commanding tone, as if forgetting who he is and talking to her young son. "Yes, yes, now, put your hand down."

Aeson raises one brow, but places his large, elegant hand flat on the counter.

The woman examines it, then pats it gently. Next, she taps his wrist with her index finger.

"Make a fist," she says.

"Huh?" Now I make a little sound.

But Aeson complies, with continuing amusement. He slowly flexes his powerful, long fingers into a fist, letting it rest on the counter surface.

The shopkeeper stares at it. "Good. You have a big, strong hand, so—big *varqooi*. Imperial *varqooi*." She then looks back at the purple dildo. "This *amrevet* toy is the perfect size—smaller than your Imperial *varqooi*, and will not cause problem for your pregnant wife. Good choice! Don't let her use anything bigger until after the baby comes! Then she can ride whatever she likes. Okay to have really big toy inside, even two—"

My mouth falls open.

But now this outrageous woman suddenly turns to me and stretches out her hand to gently pat my tummy—absolutely without my permission and unfazed by the fact that we are literally foreign royalty.

"Three, four months?" she remarks in a motherly scold. "No deep thrusting! When you put the *varqooi* toy inside, be careful, don't disturb the baby! And use a lot of sauce!"

"Oh—" I mumble. "But that's not—"

That's not scientifically accurate, I want to tell her. *That's misinformation, just nonsensical old wives' tales.*

Then it occurs to me: I'm literally talking to the epitome of an old folk wife who is giving me a well-intentioned harangue.

"And don't use bigger toys than your man's *varqooi*, understand? Okay to use big ones after baby comes out and stretches your *amreh*."

"Okay. . . ." I'm so stunned at this point that I can only nod, and I'm definitely beyond embarrassment.

"Instead of riding him, let him lick you more. Use the sauce!"

Oh . . . my . . . Gawd.

Suddenly, I want to giggle. My head is still burning, but now there's more. Crazy things are spinning inside my cranium, going round and round. . . .

Aeson's gaze meets mine, and I realize that he, too, is barely holding back laughter.

The shopkeeper does not seem to notice our state of repressed hilarity, and proceeds to wrap our ridiculous purchases with practiced care in bright fabric. And yes, even now, she's still chatting and commenting on every single one.

Finally, she puts everything inside a shopping bag—

basically, a nice cloth sack embroidered with the local Heketi folk designs, and displaying a prominent logo of the Hebu Lighthouse.

Aeson sees my shaking form, as I struggle to hold back hysterical laughter, and simply pays. I don't argue with him about using my own *iretar* credit.

"Thank you thank you, Imperial Sovereigns! Come back again! Enjoy your gifts! Enjoy tonight—remember, lick more, thrust less! More sauce, always more sauce is best—you can even warm it up—"

Aeson grabs the bag, and we practically run back through the store toward the exit, while the shopkeeper continues to cheerfully call out shameless intimacy advice in our wake.

Finally, we're out of there. Once outside, both of us burst out laughing, madly. I am nearly doubled over, and Aeson moves in to support me. I hyperventilate, and make so much noise that the Imperial guards (stationed at the doors and waiting for us all this time as we shopped) hurry toward us with minor concern.

"Oh, my gawd!" I exclaim, catching my breath (and thankfully not peeing myself in public). I grab my husband by the shoulders, pulling him closer to me so that I can whisper-scream at him without having the guards hear every word. "Aeson Kassiopei! I don't care that you might be the godlike ruler of half this planet, but if you ever do that again, I will kill you! In fact, I still might kill you when we get back home—"

In reply, Aeson chuckles, catches his breath, then laughs even deeper, wrapping one arm around my waist, at the same time as he hands off the shopping bag to the nearest guard.

"You think I'm kidding?" I whisper in his ear with absolute fierceness. "My sweet Imperial Sovereign, I'm going to *kill* you with that dildo!"

My Imperial Husband bursts out laughing again. He then continues shaking with hilarity and looks at me with delight, barely managing to utter, "Okay, as long . . . as long as you use a lot of . . . *sauce.*"

"Oh, you think it's going up your ass? Oh no, no, no-o-o-o-o," I giggle-snarl. "And *no*, there won't be pleasant lubrication, either. I'll be pounding your head with that wood—or silicone, or plastic—or whatever—right there! Right on top of your big Imperial cranium!"

WE ARRIVE BACK on our luxury *nubu depet*, and our shopping bag full of outrageous stuff is deposited in our living room by an unsuspecting Imperial guard.

It's not as if we've been walking around all that long—just to that gift shop and main street—but pregnancy makes me tired so much sooner, these days. Also, to be honest, I'm still recovering from climbing all those hundreds of steps last night. And I've just had a very pleasant but draining laughing fit.

I let out a breath of exhaustion and collapse on our overstuffed sofa. Then I sigh with pleasure born of relief at not having to move. . . .

Aeson stands a few steps away, talking on his wrist unit, most likely with our ship captain, because in moments our vessel lurches softly and begins to rise from its hover-parked location. It gains altitude gently, so that Aeson and I can watch the grand panorama of the radiant but severe landscape unfolding around us, including the cliffs and the long inlet that holds the southern portion of the Hebu Sea.

Ascending slowly in this manner, we're also reminded of the immense height of the Ancient Hebu Lighthouse. It's truly unbelievable. Even now, even after having flown hundreds of feet up in the air, we're still alongside it, observing the endless rough-hewn stones of the exterior wall flicker past us.

Finally, we reach the top and scale the crystal dome— marveling at the glittering hemisphere that sails in stately fashion just below us—and we continue flying onward into the white haze of morning.

Our direction is southwest, and our destination is Ushab, the capital of Eos-Heket.

AS WE TEMPORARILY RISE TO an altitude of the clouds, Aeson calls the kitchen for some refreshments.

"Aeson," I say, lying back against the sofa cushions. "I might be turning into a beached whale, but we really don't need to eat just yet—do we?"

I stop speaking, consider my own body, and then realize that I'm actually quite hungry.

Or likely, the baby is.

"Never mind," I say, laughing weakly at myself, "Bring it on."

Aeson smiles at me fondly and continues placing the food order to our kitchen staff.

"You want dumpling soup again?" he asks me, glancing away from his wrist device.

"Yes, please. Also, spicy pickled vegetables. And some *qvaali* to drink. I'm in a fizzy mood."

Aeson nods and continues the order.

Meanwhile, I lean forward and pick up the shopping bag full of unspeakable things from the tourist shop.

Argh! I forgot to buy proper souvenirs for my family, Dad and Gracie in particular.

Silently annoyed at myself, I rummage around the *amrevet* toys (trying very much to ignore them—at least for now) and pick out the two Hekatria divination decks. Just as I start to tear the packaging on one of them, I notice from the corner of my eye a silvery shadow on the floor near the legs of the big chair across from me.

The big silver-white cat is watching my every move with its

large golden eyes. Its ears are not flattened, but rather perked up, so it's definitely on alert but not frightened.

"Ohri!" I say in a soothing voice. "Hi, Ohri. . . ."

The cat responds to my speech by freezing in place and continuing to stare at me, unblinking.

Then, slowly, it backs away and fades, like a dear little grey-and-white ghost, out of sight.

I can no longer see it, but somehow, its invisible presence remains, filling the chamber with a curiously tangible, additional warm spirit.

It's no longer just Aeson and me in these quarters.

Now, there's three of us.

(In memory of Stevie.)

CHAPTER 15

The food arrives, and we feast while watching Hel's fierce light play on the clouds. Then I climb into our spacious bed and take a food coma nap while Aeson goes to exercise in the ship's gym.

When I wake up, there's a big ball of silvery white fur curled up on the opposite side of the bed, where Aeson's feet would normally be.

Oh, wow. . . .

Ohri decided to make himself—or herself—comfortable out in the open! That's huge progress for a feral cat, really, in such a short period of time.

I freeze, so as not to frighten the kitty, but, too late. It senses my waking movements, quickly looks up at me, then dashes from the bed and disappears once again somewhere.

Small, itty bitty, kitty steps, I think with a smile, stretching with a deep, blissful yawn.

Looks like Aeson is still at the gym.

I get up awkwardly and visit the bathroom, then return to find that our *depet* has started descending from high altitude to scenery observation level, which means, we're close to our destination. It also means there are interesting things to see outside our window.

What I first notice outside is a lot of greenery, an unrelenting, emerald carpet of forest directly below us.

And then, come the fertile grassy plains. Occasional small settlements appear, and several paved roadways emerge below, cutting through the green plains like artificial rivers.

We've left the polar-adjacent conditions of northern Eos-Heket, and are entering a zone of more temperate climate, and more population. I watch the passing landscape, mesmerized.

Aeson comes in, sweaty from running and working out, just as the afternoon light softens, and the plains fill with lengthening shadows of mauve and teal and orange-gold.

"Had a nice workout, mister?" I ask with a smile.

"Yes, very," he replies, smiling back at me. "Let me shower off."

"Okay," I say, looking at his glistening biceps and the sexy muscles of his shoulders in that sleeveless shirt he's wearing—soaked through and clinging to his bronzed skin. "Ohri the cat was sleeping on the bed just now, when I woke up."

"Really? Excellent. Definite progress." And he disappears in the bathroom. Moments later, I hear running water.

So, I turn my attention back to the view of the plains below our ship.

WHEN AESON RETURNS, he is naked except for a towel wrapped around his middle. His long hair is wet, its rare hue of true gold darkened to honey, falling down his back in careless, messy locks.

My husband looks spectacular.

I pat the bed next to me and smile suggestively at him. Okay, I just smile; I don't really know how suggestive it comes off, but I'm trying to make my eyes go all languid, and give him the "come hither" look. Short of batting my lashes like a cartoon character, I'm not sure how else to do it.

But Aeson notices my ridiculous efforts and chuckles.

He hops on the bed next to me, and leans in to kiss my neck. As he does that, I run my fingers through his luxurious damp hair.

"When do we arrive in Ushab?" I start to caress his shoulders.

"Probably in another hour. I want you to have a good leisurely view of the land before we get to the urban areas." Aeson watches me with growing intensity. He then starts undoing the very loose ribbon laces holding together the top of my dress. His warm fingers slip in and out of the dress fabric, and whenever they touch my skin, I feel frissons of electricity.

I changed into a casual, more comfortable dress before I took my nap. And I took my bra off, so my boobs are unrestrained. Yes, he's definitely looking at my chest right now. . . .

"Sounds good. What about the Oratorat?" I say in a low voice. "Did she say what time we're supposed to see her?"

Aeson pauses working on my laces for a moment, thinking. "She didn't specify. We simply need to let her know when we get there."

"Then we don't have to rush." My voice has become husky.

"No, we don't." My Imperial Husband finishes opening up the top of my dress, spreads apart the collar fabric, and buries his face in my big tits.

His jaw with its beginnings of stubble barely grazes the delicate skin of my chest. And then I feel his hot mouth. . . .

I make a soft gasp and lie back on the pillows. Meanwhile, he takes my boobs out of the dress, scoops them together, and sucks my nipples, one then the other, drawing them deeply inside his mouth—which makes me breathe loudly, each exhalation turning into a moan.

The dreamy haze of arousal starts addling my brain. I

continue to stroke his damp hair, his head busy on my breasts. I hear his own harsh breaths while my heart hammers in my chest.

Long, sensual moments later, Aeson lets go of my boobs and moves down to gently rest his cheek against my belly. He pauses, seeming to listen, then kisses my rounded stomach, and our child inside, and looks up at me. His lapis-blue eyes are languid and dreamy with a kind of fragile wonder.

No words pass between us, and no words are necessary. My breathing slows down somewhat, arousal becoming secondary, as my heart swells with love for him. . . .

After a few more moments of awe-filled mutual stillness, Aeson plants another kiss on my pregnant belly, then looks up at me again, this time with a very intense, very carnal gaze. His pupils widen, growing dark, and his mouth curves into a smile full of erotic promise.

"Gwen . . . open wide for me," he says in a deceptively quiet, deep voice, full of enough mesmerizing force that it's just short of being a *power voice*. He then starts to slide even lower, past my belly toward my crotch.

I do as I'm told, instinctively spreading my legs for him. I hitch my dress all the way up to my stomach and, underneath, I'm completely naked.

My husband puts his strong, warm hands on my inner thighs, caressing them and pushing them apart even more, and looks at me. "Should we try some *amrevet* toys, *im amrevu?*"

"No," I say at once, cringing in minor annoyance. "Just you, please."

"Are you sure?"

"Yes. I'm not in the mood for figuring out those alien powered gadgets, and I'm still quite *mad* at you for the whole thing in front of that gift shop lady."

But as I say these things, I barely manage to hold my lips in a straight line.

"Not even the sauce?" he persists, with wicked amusement.

"Especially not the sauce!" I exclaim, then sit up and grab a bunch of his damp hair and attempt to slap the Imperator of Imperial *Atlantida* upside his head.

Aeson makes a surprised sound, fends me off with one very muscular arm, backs away, and starts chuckling.

I giggle in turn.

Both of us are once again laughing, until suddenly Aeson's towel falls off. As he leans slowly toward me again, I can see his dick already twitching and rising.

I stop laughing, just like that. Knowing that it takes him mere seconds to become fully engorged and erect, arousal strikes me once more, in a powerful wave. My heart begins pounding wildly inside me.

Meanwhile, he moves down the bed, again spreading my thighs apart. He comes down over me, and I feel his hot mouth on my vulva, as he licks me a few times, in an exploratory way, light as a feather, tongue moving around and locating the clitoris.

With every warm, wet stroke, I feel a series of sharp pangs, as a flood of arousal hits me hard. Immediately, I moan, dissolving into him. . . .

He hears my undeniable response and begins moving his mouth rhythmically, using gentle suction around and over the clitoris, until I am on fire down there. . . .

"Ah! *Aeson!*" I cry out. "*A-a-ah!*"

And then, like quick summer rain, I explode in a violent, unexpected orgasm.

My womb contracts, my vaginal muscles pulse, and my hips start bucking wildly around his head. I clutch his hair with my fists, then my fingers grab his head, and pull him toward me, *into me*, as my body spasms. And he lets me.

In those moments of senseless abandon, it's as if I want to

take him, all of *him*, inside my womb and assimilate his flesh into mine.

I want him inside me, deep. . . .

When I'm done moving—waves receding, sweet peace quelling my body—I feel a gush of excessive wetness down there, the undeniable results of my release. I don't remember the last time I squirted so much during sex. . . .

My husband looks up at me with glistening lips, which he licks provocatively.

"Was it good?" he asks.

"Oh yes, very!" I sigh with languid pleasure.

Im amrevu smiles.

I smile back at him with catlike satiation.

I give myself several delicious seconds of stillness, then sit up and turn toward Aeson. "Now, your turn," I whisper, pointing at my man's obvious predicament. "Your Big Boy needs some attention—right *now*."

My husband doesn't need to be told twice. Immediately he moves in, with a leonine pounce, and this time adjusting himself over me and positioning himself at my crotch with his knees between my legs.

His big cock is swollen to its fullest, and it stands upright, so he has to use one hand to adjust it downward before entering me—for some reason, slipping inside slower than usual.

"Keep going," I say, my hands grasping his arms, drawing him closer to me, even as my breath catches with renewed arousal at the hot, hard feel of him *inside* me.

"She did say 'no deep thrusting,'" Aeson remarks, looking down at me with a shadow smile.

"Oh, please!" I mutter with sarcasm, my words in a thick, weird mixture of erotic excitement and disgust. "She also said 'lick more, thrust less!' To hell with that, I want you to go in deep!"

"Are you sure?" Aeson strokes slowly, once—in, out, filling

my insides with sharp, electric waves of need—then pauses again, as if still unconvinced. "What if the baby—"

"Crap! I want you to *pound* me!" I exclaim suddenly.

Aeson nods, smiles ruefully, then exhales, making a harsh, deep sound. His face tenses up, and now he's deadly serious, his mouth fixed in a controlled line.

And his lower body starts moving, pumping *hard*.

The angle at which he thrusts into me is still careful, still making sure not to push too much against my belly.

But oh, he is turning me to fire.

Soon, I can no longer tell apart our bodies . . . where he begins and where I end . . . how our limbs struggle and come together, fingers clawing into flesh, generating common heat, voices groaning and grunting with profound rutting effort—because my mind is not my own.

I orgasm again, and Aeson comes fiercely right after, his low baritone voice scraping the floor with a long final groan.

Then he stiffens, stops moving, and ejaculates hot inside me —so much, that it spills out and all over my thighs, and on our bed covers.

"*Varqood* . . ." he says, collapsing partially over me, and then both of us lie still for a few heartbeats in the warm, sticky mess.

"Crap . . ." I say, lying underneath him and starting to laugh. "The laundry people must really hate us. We completely missed the sheets and got this nice, fresh comforter."

"Don't worry. They're professional. They know what to expect," my husband tells me reassuringly.

"Just once," I say, giggling, "just once, can we blame it on the cat?"

CHAPTER 16

We arrive in Ushab, the capital city of Eos-Heket, flying over a sprawling urban panorama of buildings both modern and uniquely traditional.

Our *nubu depet* is an oversized luxury vessel, so once again we must sail above the normal air traffic lanes. Meanwhile, the standard hovercars and transports rush directly below us like a gleaming hive of metallic bees, filling the sky over the city.

We pass towering modern skyscrapers shaped like cylinders, with verdant rooftop gardens. These are interspersed with low and squat buildings in an intricate older style, with stone reliefs and sculpted design features. Here and there, gilded roofs sparkle in the sunset, not unlike the kind found in Poseidon. Several green parks come into view, and large sports arenas enclosed with transparent glass roofs.

Throughout all this, a river meanders, its waters appearing hazy silver or onyx-black, depending on how the light strikes it. Aeson tells me this is Ben-Ushab, an offshoot of a much larger river called Ashraha, on the shore of which the city lies.

"Ashraha is the largest river on the upper continent. The second largest river is in Imperial *Atlantida*, on the northeastern side," Aeson says, standing next to me as we stare at the landscape below from our observation window. We're still in our disheveled, semi-naked condition after our vigorous sex, and my inner thighs and buttocks are sticky with his ultra-potent Imperial *phietei* that has dripped down my legs. . . .

"Good to know," I say, lightly stroking his upper arm and thinking about all that running water, and how nice it would be to dunk myself in it, right about now. *Why does making love result in such a mess?*

"Notice, I didn't say it was the largest river on the planet," my lovely pedantic husband elaborates with a faint smile.

I can't help but admire the beautiful lean hollows of his cheekbones, the angles of his jaw. Then my gaze continues downward, along his neck, his strong shoulders, sculpted pectorals and abs, his beautiful bronzed muscles glistening with sex sweat. He and I are *both* desperately in need of another shower. . . .

"So, what's the largest river on the planet?" I humor him because, to be honest, I'm loving this trivia as much as he does, apparently. We're both nerds.

"That would be the river Teramazd, on the lower continent. It's located primarily in New Deshret, though it ends far north in Chimir, its mouth flowing into the Gagik Sea. A huge river network, actually, with many offshoots and distributaries."

"Something else we should see?" I ask.

"We certainly could, at some point in our travels. Teramazd is very impressive."

At that point Aeson's wrist unit rings with an incoming message. It's from the Oratorat, and we are invited to attend an evening event organized specifically for us.

"How nice of her," I say, pulling together the fabric of my dress top while trying to stuff one of my naked breasts inside the loosened bodice.

Aeson raises one brow with amusement at my efforts. "Nice . . . well, yes."

"What?"

Aeson turns the focus of his unabashedly lustful gaze from my chest to my face and leans in closer. I can see his humorous energy rising, judging by the heightened sparkle in his eyes. "You need to know this, so I might as well tell you. Kephasa Sewu, as you might recall from your several encounters with that woman, is a sterling individual, an excellent ally to *Atlantida*, and a fine conversationalist. Indeed, as the Oratorat, it is literally her defining government position—to *speak for* the people. But . . . ultimately, she only has one thing on her mind—*business*. The most excruciating kind of business imaginable. Her invitation is gracious, but, wait and see . . . it's all going to devolve into a tedious 'little work meeting' for me, while you'll be pleasantly distracted and entertained by her minions."

"Poor Imperial you," I run my fingers up his arm, continuing to stroke gently. "Can you manage to avoid it?"

Aeson smiles. "Not a chance. It would be impolite to our gracious hosts. But you could rescue me at the right moment."

"I could. I'll remind her we're on our Amrevet days."

"Not good enough. She's insidious and relentless in her ability to turn all pleasure into productivity. You would have to grab onto me with both hands—like this—or you'll be pulled into the meeting too. And then, *im amrevu*, right in the middle of a festive occasion, you'll be faced with probing questions about supply chain management logistics, regional economic resources, public services, and end up discussing border legislation and infrastructure for at least an hour, making you wish you were getting dental work instead."

I giggle.

"You laugh now," Aeson says, wiggling his brows. "But you will, at some point, beg for sweet death to take you—once she starts describing public sewer excavation permits, guidelines for depths of trenches, and road work projects she has in mind for connecting freight routes between Eos-Heket and Imperial *Atlantida*. As you can imagine, she is excellent at her job, and is eager to take it out on others."

I giggle even harder.

Aeson picks up my hands, and turns them wrist side up. He then places a very soft, very sensual kiss on the pulse point of each wrist, left then right. "Let's clean up and get dressed," he says. And then he gives my rear end a very light but lingering squeeze.

OUR *NUBU DEPET* descends and hover parks in a wide empty lot behind a modern complex of tall buildings near the city center.

According to Aeson, they are the government complex of Ushab, including the Oratorium, which is the equivalent of a parliament building.

While we wait, watching the teal sunset extinguish itself into evening and more and more artificial illumination fill the urban panorama, our captain calls to inform the local government officials that we have arrived. Soon, we can see from the windows an approaching small cavalcade of hovercars in black and silver chrome, ready to escort us to our destination.

At this point, Aeson and I have showered, and are dressed in semi-formal wear. I'm wearing a dramatic black evening gown that hangs with loose elegance over my pregnant body, and sparkling chandelier earrings with deep blue Pegasus Blood stones (Aeson's recent present) to perfectly match my Wedding ring. My hair is up in a simple earth-style knot. My feet however are in sensible flats.

Aeson is in a dark blue jacket with fine gold trim on the simple lapels, without the heavy wide *wesekh* collar of state. It emphasizes his elegant wide shoulders, with a cream-white silk shirt underneath, dark pants, and polished shoes. His long hair, in all its golden Kassiopei glory, falls loosely down his powerful, straight back. Yes, he looks understated, compared to the usual Imperial regalia that he's obliged to wear for public and state occasions, but is impressive nevertheless.

Such a glorious, beautiful man, what else would he be? I think, with a little joyful frisson of marvel that I sometimes get when looking at him. It's an out-of-body sensation of awe, as I consider my life circumstances. And as always, immediately afterward, my heart constricts almost painfully with love.

"I hope we're not underdressed," I whisper to Aeson, but he merely encloses my hand with his large, warm fingers, in reassurance.

We exit the *nubu depet* down the gentle ramp, followed by the Imperial guards, and are immediately met with a blast of cool evening air. Gracious uniformed officials in dark red and mahogany-brown, the national colors of Eos-Heket, are lined up to greet us, a few steps away, with the hovering cars waiting directly behind them.

"*Wixameret*, Imperial Sovereign and Sovereign Lady of Imperial *Atlantida*." A tall woman in front of the line steps forward with a sharp nod that is not quite a bow, speaking flawless *Atlanteo*. "May I escort you to the reception? The Honorable Oratorat Kephasa Sewu is expecting you."

"Thank you. We are looking forward to seeing the Oratorat," Aeson replies smoothly.

And we get in the first car.

MINUTES LATER—PARDON me, daydreams—we traverse the large airfield lot and arrive at the front entrance of the nearest building, seeming to be of an older architectural style, with a distinctive raised staircase of beige and bisque marble. It culminates in a grand entrance with carved doors of dark sienna-brown wood inlaid with contrasting pale stone reliefs bearing the imagery of mythic beasts and curling serpentine creatures reminiscent of dragons.

I stare at them, thinking of Chinese-style dragons from Earth, as the doors are opened before us by uniformed guards. Our own Imperial guards stay behind, here at the doors, handing us into the secure care of the Heketi officials and the thoroughly vetted gathering that awaits.

Aeson takes my hand, and we go up the slippery stone stairs, polished by decades, and possibly centuries of use. Once inside, we are met with an ocean of lights and a grand assembly hall packed with people.

The chamber is elegant but somewhat severe in comparison to its sculpted exterior, with ivory-colored walls, a lofty tiered ceiling, and four corners marked by spare colonnades, but no other distinctive elements of décor. The floor is smooth polished stone in shades of mauve and cream, and large orb-lights float overhead to provide sufficient illumination.

The difference between Eos-Heket and Imperial *Atlantida* is immediate. There are no thrones in this assembly chamber, only a perimeter of comfortable seats along each wall, interspersed with refreshment buffet tables. Light instrumental mood music reminiscent of modern Earth jazz blended with Hindustani folk dance is playing over speakers, without a live orchestra in sight. People are dressed in semi-formal, festive contemporary wear, not unlike what I've seen in Poseidon, but far simpler. Even at their most formal they are closer to the attire of Low Court.

We are announced by an amplified voice, so that all heads turn in our direction. And then I recognize the Oratorat herself, part of a conversation group near the center of the hall. At once, she detaches herself from the group and heads in our direction.

The Honorable Oratorat Kephasa Sewu is a middle-aged woman with hawkish features, lean and bony, handsome instead of beautiful. Her face is graced by a fierce aquiline nose, very dark eyebrows over deep-set brown eyes, and dark brown hair gathered in a severe knot with fine gold netting. She wears a floor-length mahogany red dress with black trim, and sensible shoes like myself.

A prominent sculpted gold ring with the Eos-Heket seal of state encircles the index finger of her right hand. The ring is curiously attached with a gold chain to a wide gold bracelet which, I assume, is part of her official attire. I can ask Aeson about it later. . . .

"Welcome to Ushab, Imperial Sovereign Aeson Kassiopei, and Sovereign Lady Gwen," the Oratorat says with a light smile, encompassing us both in her greeting. And then her gaze falls on my prominent baby bump which is now definitely a belly. "I hope your visit of Eos-Heket has been pleasant so far."

"Very much so, indeed," Aeson replies with a friendly expression. "We thank you for giving us the opportunity to experience at leisure your beautiful nation with its natural and man-made wonders."

"It's been truly wonderful, thank you so much, Oratorat," I say warmly. "I couldn't imagine how surprising and glorious the scenery would be! And the historical sites, such as the Ancient Hebu Lighthouse—"

"Ah yes, you've been to the Lighthouse; it's a marvel indeed, our most famous unique heritage landmark," the Oratorat says, and her smile deepens with pride. "Of course, it's quite a climb. Fortunately, for a woman in your condition there's an elevator, which I'm sure you were relieved to utilize in order to avoid the more-than-a-thousand stairs—"

"Oh, no, I climbed it," I say with a twinge of silly pride in my tone. And I'm rewarded with the Oratorat's expression of genuine surprise.

"What? Seriously?" The older woman looks from me to Aeson.

My Imperial Husband raises one brow quizzically and nods.

"Yes, she did. She refused the elevator and climbed every single stair. I could barely keep up. Don't forget, my incredible Wife is a Games Champion."

"Yes, I recall. Remarkable," the Oratorat says, looking at me in continued estimation. "Personally, I would've been too anxious for the child's wellbeing to attempt that climb. . . . Not my business, of course. I hope you take no offense. I'm a mother of three, and my process was never easy, while you are young and in superb health. But—enough of such things, we are here to enjoy the evening."

"Of course," I reply, considering her more closely in turn. "I admit, I'm not sure why I felt I had to climb it on my own, but it was something I was moved to do. . . . I did take many, many rest stops. But oh, the view on the top, in the crystal dome chamber, is amazing."

The Oratorat's serious demeanor transforms into a smile. "I cannot argue with that."

Suddenly she nods, as if recalling herself, and turns around, casting glances behind her. She then beckons several people from the nearest grouping to approach us.

"Before I invite you to take your seats and try our most delicious Heketi refreshments," the Oratorat says to Aeson and me, "I want to reassure you, there will be no formal matters of state tonight, no introductions of our ministry officials. Everyone is aware you're on a personal pleasure visit, and this is just relaxing entertainment. However, I must *casually* introduce you, our esteemed Imperial guests, to several of our exemplary citizens. They've been invited to attend this evening specifically for this reason. I believe you will be rather pleased. . . ."

I stare curiously, and even Aeson appears intrigued.

The group of people who were called come up to us, all appearing quite young, and conservatively dressed. They are all smiling with a kind of shy mischief that I cannot quite fathom, until. . . .

I happen to look at one of the young women and suddenly, quite impossibly, *recognize* her. I *know* those brave blue eyes, the stubborn angular jaw, the somewhat frail, but no longer quite so skinny figure. She's gotten a little taller, and gotten rid of her light brown bangs that covered her eyebrows and forehead . . . . Now her hair is neatly pulled back into a tight, businesslike knot at the nape of her neck.

She is smartly dressed in an elegant, dark olive jacket and matching slim skirt, heels, and has two sparkling stud earrings, giving her a very mature, very worldly look.

"*Zoe?*" I break into English, dropping my jaw in amazement. "Oh my God! Is that you, Zoe Blatt?"

The young woman's face lights up. In those few seconds I see her expression dissolve into a huge smile, then a wide laughing grin.

"Gwen! Yes! I knew you'd remember me! Our Semi-Finals team from L.A.!"

"Of course I remember you! Hell, yes! How could I ever forget?" I exclaim, forgetting myself in a different way and using strong language before the Oratorat (who merely looks amused and very pleased, and maybe not quite fluent enough to know such nuances of English). "I can't believe this! What are you doing here? And, oh—you Qualified!"

Zoe continues smiling widely, nodding at me. "Yup, Qualified, amazingly. Long story short, made it onto the shuttle, then the ark-ship, then, when we arrived in Atlantis, they assigned me to Ushab, here in Eos-Heket. I'm a Heketi resident now!"

"Oh wow! *Wow!*" At this point I've lost all sense of caution, dropped any semblance of public Imperial Protocol, and forgotten the need to be the polite face of *Atlantida*. In fact, I think I just involuntarily regressed almost two whole years, to a younger me . . . back to Earth, the Semi-Finals in L.A., then the NQC in Colorado where I last saw Zoe, fleetingly among the crowds in the airfield, on that fateful morning as we were boarding the shuttles heading into the Finals. Right now, it feels like my facial muscles have dissolved with stupid joy, and I'm slightly shaking. "I am so happy, Zoe! So happy to see you okay and *alive*, and here of all places!"

I glance at Aeson briefly, and see that he has also relaxed his usual controlled expression. He watches us with a warm, easy smile.

As for the Oratorat—she nods and finally interrupts our reunion. "I'm glad to see this meeting has worked out even better than expected. These fine individuals, all selected for their excellent progress in their newly chosen professions and contributions to Eos-Heket society, are all former Earth refugees, and now full-fledged citizens of our nation. Not just residents, but *citizens*, for we do not make it a policy to withhold full citizenship—by birth or naturalization—from any Heketi woman, man, or child."

It's a gentle jab at Imperial *Atlantida's* citizenship caste policy, but at this point Aeson tactfully ignores it, and so do I.

"Oh!" I say with wonder, now glancing closely at the other young people in the group. "So wonderful to meet all of you!"

"Very well, I'll leave you to it, Sovereign Lady Gwen. As you can see, our gathering here tonight is quite relaxed, not a formal state visit, so please enjoy yourself, circulate among our guests, and be sure to drink and eat *sufficiently*—we have quite a feast laid out for you, very healthy options too." The Oratorat says to me with a meaningful glance at my pregnant belly.

Then she turns to my husband. "Now, Imperial Sovereign Aeson, while this beautiful Gebi reunion takes place, you and I might meet for a brief moment and discuss a few things we talked about previously—"

I glance at Aeson quickly, and see him giving me an amused look of *I told you so.* "Of course, Oratorat," he responds graciously.

"Shall we go and find a seat near the refreshment tables?" Oratorat Kephasa Sewu says, and takes Aeson by the elbow to lead him with determination in the direction of the faraway seats and buffet.

I remain next to Zoe, in the circle of Earth refugees. Everyone is smiling at me, and now that it's just us, everyone loosens up.

"Sovereign Lady Gwen—" one girl begins, but I interrupt her.

"Please, it's just Gwen. No formalities needed now!"

"Okay, Gwen," the girl continues. "We haven't met, and I wasn't there, but I remember some people at the NQC talking about you and what happened in Los Angeles. That's when they started calling you Shoelace Girl?"

"Oh yeah, that was way before everything," Zoe puts in. "Our original Shoelace Girl team!"

I smile and continue shaking slightly and move my head in disbelief. "Yes, all that. And speaking of—any idea what happened to Jared Holder and Ethan Jamerson? Are they here too, by any chance?"

I am tentatively hopeful as I ask this . . . Fact is, I've been too terrified to look into the fates of the members of the original Earth Team Lark. So, I kept postponing it.

Afraid of what I might find out. Afraid to learn that they all died. . . .

Maybe it's the memory of Sarah Thornwald's dead body, forever lurking in the back of my mind, always tied together with that other death, that of the nameless Blue girl, whose killing was *my first*. I caused it, no matter how indirectly. And in the weird way of trauma, my subconscious came to associate all of them with these Qualification horrors. . . .

Of course, then came other traumas, compounded; other worse horrors of the Games, the alien war, the impeding destruction of Earth, my Mom. . . .

No, stop.

I slam the floodgates of the past shut.

"Not sure," Zoe replies. "I don't think they're in Ushab, at least. I was thinking I could look up the official records, but . . . kind of didn't want to, for a long time—was afraid of what I might find out."

I nod, my expression growing serious. "Same here . . . exactly." I take a deep breath. "I'm sorry, but I didn't even try to look for any of you three. I kept telling myself I would check eventually, later, someday, but—"

Zoe shakes her head, hesitates in some kind of uncertainty. Then she puts her hand lightly on my arm. "I know. It's okay. I understand completely. Like I said, I'm the same way. Or, I was. But, being in the legal profession now—which I'll tell you all about in a minute—I did finally use the legal resources at my disposal to look them up, recently."

"Oh! You did?"

Zoe pauses. "And I found nothing. There is no record of them on Ushab, or anywhere else on Eos-Heket, and when I tried to dig deeper, they aren't on *Atlantida* either. Nor is there a record of them being on the ark-ships."

I feel a sharp jolt of painful emotion.

It must be very obvious on my face, because Zoe again pats my arm and squeezes it. "Gwen, no," she says gently. "It doesn't necessarily mean they're not okay. We *don't* know. They could simply be back on Earth, not having passed the Finals Qualification."

Or they died in the underwater tunnels. . . .

Because, what other way is there to not pass the Finals? I think. George's situation was somewhat unusual, in that his low Team score disqualified him.

"I know what you're thinking," Zoe persists. "Don't go there. Remember, tons of people got all the way through the tunnels under the Atlantic to that central cavern, but still didn't make it up to the shuttles, for one reason or another. And they simply ended up going home. I'm sure Jared and Ethan had the skills to get that far, and are back home safely on Earth right now."

"You're absolutely right," I speak up at last. "Maybe I'll look into it now. I can ask Aeson, my husband—"

"That's right!" Zoe smiles again. "You have the means to take it all the way to the top! I still can't believe what you've accomplished! The Imperatris of Imperial *Atlantida*! Winner of those wild Games of yours, not to mention the role you played in saving Earth from the asteroid, and then the alien war—"

"Please, don't remind me," I shake my head with a rueful smile, then sigh and place my own hand on Zoe's. "May I give you a hug?" I ask softly.

Zoe's mouth parts. "Are you kidding? I was the one worried if it was okay to touch you, the Imperatris! Like, was I overstepping just now by touching your hand?" And she steps forward and puts her arms around me, awkwardly at first, then holds me in a firm embrace. "I'm not squishing your baby, am I?" she whispers, laughing softly.

"No, you're not," I say with warmth, as I rest against her cheek, not caring what anyone else in this hall might think.

"Oh, my gawd, you're having a royal baby . . ." Zoe speaks near my ear. "I can't believe I'm hugging you and you're here!"

We come apart, and smile at each other, locked in a strange microcosm of memories and moments of past intensity.

Someone clears their throat.

"This is so cool that you know each other," an Earthie guy says, looking at the other former Earth refugees.

In those few minutes of being engrossed with Zoe, I've almost forgotten the others.

"So sorry," I say, looking at all of them. "Not ignoring you, I promise, just having an unexpected awesome reunion with a friend. Hey, how about we all find some chairs and go talk and get acquainted?"

And off we all go, as a group, toward the nearest seating area and the buffet tables. As we walk through the crowds, I nod and smile at everyone we pass, and the Heketi natives nod and smile back at me, in a casual and friendly manner. They are not nobility (for that is not the Heketi way), just people who have done well for themselves and likely achieved much in their professional lives.

Briefly, I glance around to see if I can locate Aeson. He is off in the distance, seated in a semicircle with the Oratorat and a few serious looking government officials—definitely engrossed in a "meeting."

At some point this evening I will have to "rescue him" as promised, but not just yet.

First, I am going to indulge my Gebi soul and commune with my fellow refugees.

WE SIP SPARKLING DRINKS, munch on tasty savory and sweet treats of Eos-Heket, and sit around reminiscing. We talk about *us*—here, now, on Atlantis. Everything we've been through. And then, as time goes on, we dare to talk about the loved ones we've left behind on Earth.

I discover that these young men and women come from all walks of life, having chosen fascinating occupations. Zoe tells me she is an apprentice Arbiter, on her way to becoming a legal professional. One of the guys, Chen Jia Hao, from the Henan Province in China, with a strong Mandarin accent in English, has been signed on as a player by one of the biggest professional skyball teams in Eos-Heket. Martin Connor, from Canada, is working for a science research facility specializing in quantum orichalcum tech. Adelina Carrasco, a young woman originally from Spain, is an artist and designer, incorporating Earth folk art patterns into housewares and home décor for an urban project firm in Ushab. Janet Bellor, from Connecticut, USA, a petite girl with dark brown skin and thick curls, is teaching English and several other Earth languages to the locals.

There are others, and I'm almost overwhelmed hearing about them and their personal stories. And what impresses me further is that now they're all proficient in *Heketeo*, the Heketi language, in addition to *Atlanteo*, the common Atlantis planetary lingua franca that they (along with me and all the rest of us refugees) started to learn on the ark-ships.

At some point, Zoe again taps me on the arm and takes me aside, as we get up to refill our drinks from the bursting buffet table right behind us.

"Gwen, there is something I have for you," she says, pouring a sparkling rosy-peach liquid into my glass. "It's a small gift, or loan . . . on behalf of one of our antiquities museums for which I do legal consulting work. I was meeting with Ayvedia Kohatu, the director of the Eos-Heket Historical Assets Foundation last night, and she asked me to pass it on to you, to hand to your father, Professor Charles Lark."

"Oh, really?" I take the glass, and we return to our seats.

Zoe reaches for her handbag resting on the floor and takes out a small box. "Here it is."

I take the little box from her and put down my glass. "May I open it?"

Zoe nods. "Please do. I believe this present is completely informal. An ancient trinket, but nothing out of the ordinary in terms of rarity or value—so, not that big of a deal. The director has been corresponding with Professor Lark, so he's probably expecting this. Anyway, she thinks that she found something that might be relevant to the latest research projects based on recent events. Specifically, the archeological finds inside the ancient ship graveyard on Arlenari, a.k.a. the Ghost Moon."

Now my curiosity is piqued. I unlock a tiny latch and open the box. Inside, on a bed of black satin fabric lies what appears to be a burnished gold bracelet. "How pretty," I say, taking it from its resting place. On second look, it's not gold, but tarnished orichalcum. The dull antique surface patina reflects specks of grey and gold. . . .

I turn it this and that way, and, upon closer examination, the surface of the bracelet has a simple geometric design, etched in faint, barely visible grooves that must've been worn down over the centuries. And then I notice that it's actually some kind of lettering.

Unfamiliar, alien symbols or hieroglyphs run all round the bracelet on the outside, and the same characters repeat on the inside. "Oh," I say. "Is that Heketi writing?"

Zoe shakes her head. "Nope. She told me it's something more ancient. Classical *Atlanteo*."

"I see. What does it say?"

Zoe smiles. "That's supposed to be the interesting part. It says '*Eos-Heket-Semiram*.' And then it says something else that the director and her experts can't seem to decipher. She's hoping that Professor Lark might have better luck, since he works directly with some of the top linguists specializing in Classical *Atlanteo*."

"Semiram!" I recall the name of the ancient poet who wrote *The Semiram Cycle*, the book of children's stories that Princess Manala keeps in her library. I also recall how we all speculated that it could somehow be related to the ancient scribe Semmi whose written scroll artifacts we found. All in all, my Dad and his colleagues at the Imperial Poseidon Museum will go nuts over this thing.

"Yes, exactly, '*Semiram*.' I remember reading several articles in the news about the various details of the discoveries, when it was all happening," Zoe says. "And later, that popular book which was everywhere, what was it—*Arlenari's Diary*. It mentioned another, similar name."

I smile and nod, holding the bracelet in my fingers.

It feels warm suddenly. . . .

But no, it's just my imagination. What I feel is the frisson of scientific curiosity, of ancient history tugging at me.

I carefully put the bracelet back inside the box and close the lid.

"Oh, I almost forgot," Zoe adds. "There's supposed to be a second bracelet just like this one, with the same exact design, or maybe very similar, in another national museum, in Ubasti. And they can't figure out the entirety of the inscription either."

"Ubasti?"

"Yup. They were going through the databases of ancient stuff all around Atlantis, and good thing their inventories are linked online. They found this duplicate bracelet in an archive in Ubasti."

"This is fascinating, and I know for a fact my Dad is going to love it. Thank you!" I say.

Zoe looks pleased.

WE CHAT and laugh for at least another hour, and I invite all the Earth refugees to contact me anytime in Imperial *Atlantida* and keep in touch. Zoe promises to call and visit, and finally I get up, to enact my promise to Aeson.

Looking across the room just now, I can see my Imperial Husband is still stuck in a serious conversation with the Oratorat and the same exact group of her government colleagues. Even from here, their intense focus seems abysmally out of place among the festivity.

Poor Aeson. . . .

I make my way through the jovial crowds toward them and stop, smiling politely. Aeson looks up, his expression composed, seeming almost relaxed, and utterly polite. Only I, who know him so well, can see the utmost *weariness* in his eyes.

"My apologies, everyone," I say. "Sorry to interrupt—Aeson,

I feel a little tired and it's been a lovely evening, but I really need to rest. . . . The baby, you know." And I pat my abdomen.

The Oratorat immediately stops their conversation and goes into motherly mode. "Of course! Go, please, go rest, immediately! You mustn't overtire yourself," she says, fussing like an older relative. "Imperial Sovereign—Aeson, my dear—we'll continue this later, now please attend to your Wife and child, at once. *Nefero niktos!*"

And we are practically shooed out of the hall.

AESON MAINTAINS HIS HIGHLY CONTROLLED, neutral public expression as we exit the building, where our Imperial guards immediately surround us. He only gives me meaningful glances and squeezes my hand throughout our brief Heketi formal escort car ride to our *nubu depet*.

It's only when we walk up the ramp and the doors close around us, that he lets out a deep breath and starts laughing. "*Bashtooh!* That excellent woman nearly destroyed me. It was just as excruciating as usual," he says, rubbing his forehead. "I need a drink—or something else to relax me. What took you so long?"

I tell him about the engrossing conversations I've had with my fellow Gebi. "Sorry, completely lost track of the time, especially talking with Zoe," I explain guiltily, as we head to our own luxurious quarters.

And then, plopping down on our overstuffed sofa, I show him the box with the ancient orichalcum bracelet that Zoe gave me.

Aeson sits down next to me, takes out the bracelet and examines it closely. "It's definitely Classical *Atlanteo*, what little of it you can make out. Badly worn and faded. They'll need to micro-scan it to make certain of some of these characters."

I tell him about the existence of a nearly identical, second bracelet. And then a tantalizing thought comes to me.

"Hey," I whisper, leaning against *im amrevu*'s strong, warm shoulder. "Since we're traveling around the world anyway, can we go to Ubasti ourselves and ask to look at that other bracelet?"

"Hm-m-m. We could. Let me think about it." Aeson wraps one arm around me from the back, and strokes my neck lightly with his fingers, sending delicious tingles down my skin.

In response, I place my own hand on his thigh. Then I slide it craftily toward the bulge in his pants . . . which immediately comes alive, hardening underneath the fabric, as soon as my naughty fingers close over it.

As I continue to hold him *there*, the Sovereign Lord of Imperial *Atlantida* lets out a groan and turns to stare at me with instant, raw intensity.

"Really? You need to think about it? What if I took the Big Boy out for a ride?" I whisper, slowly, *firmly* moving over him with my palm. "What will you think then?"

Aeson sucks in air harshly. He then gathers himself together long enough to tap his wrist unit and speak in a hoarse, low voice, barely on the verge of control: "Set course to Ubasti."

I laugh and begin to undo his pants.

End of Amrevet Days One

Continued in Volume Two

Want to start from the beginning?
Catch up with your free copy of **QUALIFY**,
book one of The Atlantis Grail!

Don't miss another book by Vera Nazarian!

Subscribe to the mailing list
to be notified when the next books
by Vera Nazarian are available.
veranazarian.com/signup.html

We promise not to spam you or chit-chat, only
make book release and insider news announcements.

Want to talk about it with other fans?
Join the fun at . . .
The Atlantis Grail Fan Discussion Forum
atlantisgrail.proboards.com

OTHER BOOKS BY VERA NAZARIAN

Lords of Rainbow
Dreams of the Compass Rose
Salt of the Air
The Perpetual Calendar of Inspiration
The Clock King and the Queen of the Hourglass
Mayhem at Grant-Williams High (YA)
The Duke in His Castle
After the Sundial
Mansfield Park and Mummies
Northanger Abbey and Angels and Dragons
Pride and Platypus: Mr. Darcy's Dreadful Secret
Vampires are from Venus, Werewolves are from Mars

Cobweb Bride Trilogy:
Cobweb Bride
Cobweb Empire
Cobweb Forest

The Atlantis Grail:
Qualify (Book One)
Compete (Book Two)
Win (Book Three)
Survive (Book Four)

The Atlantis Grail Novella Series
Aeson: Blue
Aeson: Black

The Atlantis Grail Superfan Extras
The Atlantis Grail Companion
People of The Atlantis Grail

(Forthcoming)

Dawn of the Atlantis Grail (TAG Prequel Series)
Eos (Book One)

Dea (Book Two)
Niktos (Book Three)
Ghost (Book Four)
Starlight (Book Five)

The Atlantis Grail:
The Book of Everything (Book Five)

The Atlantis Grail Novella Series
Xelio: Red
Brie: Red

The Atlantis Grail Superfan Extras
The Atlantis Grail Zodiac

Thank you for your support!

ABOUT THE AUTHOR

Vera Nazarian is a two-time Nebula Award® Finalist, a Dragon Award 2018 Finalist, and a member of Science Fiction and Fantasy Writers Association.

As a double refugee, after immigrating from the USSR during the Cold War, and then escaping from the Civil War in Lebanon (by way of Greece), she spent 35 years in Los Angeles, California. She now lives with many wacky cats in a small town in Vermont, and uses her Armenian sense of humor and her Russian sense of suffering to bake conflicted pirozhki and make art.

Vera sold her first story at 17, and has been published in numerous anthologies and magazines, honorably mentioned in Year's Best volumes, and translated into at least eight languages.

She made her novelist debut with the critically acclaimed *Dreams of the Compass Rose* (2002), followed by *Lords of Rainbow* (2003). Her novella *The Clock King and the Queen of the Hourglass* made the 2005 Locus Recommended Reading List. Her debut collection *Salt of the Air* contains the 2007 Nebula Award-nominated "The Story of Love." Other work includes the 2008 Nebula Finalist novella *The Duke in His Castle*, science fiction collection *After the Sundial* (2010), *The Perpetual Calendar of Inspiration* (2010), three Jane Austen parodies, *Mansfield Park and Mummies* (2009), *Northanger Abbey and Angels and Dragons* (2010), and *Pride and Platypus: Mr. Darcy's Dreadful Secret* (2012), all part of her *Supernatural Jane Austen Series*, a parody of self-help and supernatural relationships advice, *Vampires are from Venus, Werewolves are from Mars: A Comprehensive Guide to Attracting Supernatural Love* (2012), *Cobweb Bride Trilogy* (2013), bestselling series *The Atlantis Grail*, now optioned for film, which includes *Qualify* (2014), *Compete* (2015), *Win* (2017), and *Survive* (2020), novellas *Aeson: Blue* (2021), *Aeson: Black* (2022), fan guides *The Atlantis Grail Companion* (2021), and *People of the Atlantis Grail* (2023).

In addition to being a writer, philosopher, and award-winning artist, she is also the publisher of Norilana Books.

Official website: https://www.veranazarian.com

Get on my Mailing List! https://www.veranazarian.com/signup.html

Author Direct Store: https://www.veranazarianbooks.com

TAG Fan Discussion Forum: https://atlantisgrail.proboards.com/

Astra Daimon and Shoelace Girls (Facebook fan group):

https://www.facebook.com/groups/adasg/

The Atlantis Grail – SPOILERS (Facebook fan group):

https://www.facebook.com/groups/tag2spoilers

TAG official website: https://www.theatlantisgrail.com/

TAG Fandom website: https://www.tag.fan

Patreon (Adult 18+): https://patreon.com/VeraNazarian

Ream (Adult, 18+): https://reamstories.com/veranazarian

Norilana Books: https://www.norilana.com

BlueSky: https://bsky.app/profile/veranazarian.bsky.social

X: https://x.com/Norilana

Facebook: https://www.facebook.com/VeraNazarian

TikTok: https://www.tiktok.com/@veranazarian

Instagram: https://www.instagram.com/vera_nazarian/

YouTube Channel: https://www.youtube.com/veranazarian-tag

ACKNOWLEDGMENTS

There are so many of you whose unwavering, loving support helped me bring this book to life. My gratitude is boundless, and I thank you with all my heart!

To my absolutely brilliant first readers, advisors, topic experts, editors, proofreaders, fandom moderators, TAG Con Committee members and friends, Elizabeth Logotheti, Ellen Jauregui Contard, Harriet Bennett, Heather Dryer, Kerry Vosswinkel, Mary C. Sellar, Nancy Huett, Nydia Fernandez Burdick, Ricki Bristow, Roby James, Shelley Bruce, Susan Franzblau, Teri N. Sears, and West Yarbrough McDonough.

A special profound thanks to the wonderful Chris Marble for immense and timely support, going above and beyond, during complicated times.

To my wonderful producer Richard Joel of 405 Productions who is working hard to make the film project a reality.

To all the amazing and hardworking ConCom volunteers of our annual TAG Con convention.

To the lovely and wonderful group of Vermont writers and friends, Anne Stuart, Ellen Jareckie, Jeanne Miller, Lina Gimble, and Valerie Gillen, and to my dear friends in more distant places, Lisa Silverthorne and Patricia Duffy Novak.

To all the wonderful and enthusiastic members of the "Astra Daimon and Shoelace Girls" Facebook group, "The Atlantis Grail - SPOILERS" Facebook group, and the official TAG Discussion Forum on ProBoards.

To my Patreon and Ream supporters, thank you, one and all, from the bottom of my heart, you are the absolute best! Special shoutout to Joanne Utrera for Imperial Kassiopei Tier Support.

To my awesome and fabulous Wattpad friends and fans who keep re-reading each TAG preview chapter and making me smile, laugh, and otherwise delight in your hilarious, stunning, amazing, and insightful responses to the story! Thank you immensely!

If I've forgotten or missed anyone, the fault is mine; please know that I love and appreciate you all.

Finally, I would like to thank all of you dear reader friends, who decided to take my hand and step into my world of The Atlantis Grail.

My deepest thanks to all for your support!

Before you go, you are kindly invited to leave a
review of this book!

Reviews are a wonderful way to help the author! They are also an exciting opportunity to share your honest thoughts with other readers, so **please post yours**, in as many places as possible, including TikTok and Instagram!

Scan Code for Linktree.

www.ingramcontent.com/pod-product-compliance
Lightning Source LLC
Chambersburg PA
CBHW020638250626
47154CB00008B/2725